The Flags of War

The Flags
of War

John Wilson

KIDS CAN PRESS

KCP Fiction is an imprint of Kids Can Press

Kids Can Press acknowledges the financial support of the Government of Ontario, through the Ontario Media Development Corporation's Ontario Book Initiative, the Ontario Arts Council; the Canada Council for the Arts; and the Government of Canada, through the BPIDP, for our publishing activity.

Published in Canada by
Kids Can Press Ltd.
29 Birch Avenue
Toronto, ON M4V 1E2

Published in the U.S. by
Kids Can Press Ltd.
2250 Military Road
Tonawanda, NY 14150

www.kidscanpress.com

Edited by Charis Wahl
Designed by Carolyn Sebestyen
Cover designed by Karen Powers

Printed and bound in Canada

CM 04 0 9 8 7 6 5 4 3 2 1
CM PA 04 0 9 8 7 6 5 4 3 2 1

National Library of Canada Cataloguing in Publication Data

Wilson, John (John Alexander), 1951–
    The flags of war / John Wilson.

ISBN 1-55337-567-X (bound).   ISBN 1-55337-568-8 (pbk.)

1. United States — History — Civil War, 1861–1865 — Juvenile fiction.
2. Fugitive slaves — Juvenile fiction. 3. Canada — History — 1841–1867 —
    Juvenile fiction. I. Title.

PS8595.I5834F53 2004   jC813'.54   C2003-906833-1

Kids Can Press is a *Corus*™ Entertainment company

For Colin Campbell, who first showed me
that the stories in history could be fun

The flags of war like storm-birds fly,
  The charging trumpets blow;
Yet rolls no thunder in the sky,
  No earthquake strives below.

And, calm and patient, Nature keeps
  Her ancient promise well,
Though o'er her bloom and greenness sweeps
  The battle's breath of hell.

from "The Battle Autumn of 1862"
— John Greenleaf Whittier

PROLOGUE

April 16, 1746
Culloden Moor, Scotland

The heavy black cannonball bounced twice over the spongy mat of heather before decapitating the man to Rory McGregor's left. Rory glanced down at the shattered, bloodstained pile that moments before had been a living human being. He had a vague impression of an unkempt, unwashed scarecrow dressed in tartan rags, but that could have described any of the five thousand Highlanders gathered on Culloden Moor that Wednesday afternoon. Rory was not shocked by the sight of the mutilated body — there had been far too many for that. He was simply glad it was not him.

In front of Rory, a rolling wall of dark, acrid smoke allowed only brief glimpses of the red-coated English soldiers four hundred paces away. They were standing at attention in rows, three deep, and each carried a musket topped with a long bayonet. Scattered bodies lay on the heather, but the Scottish cannons, long ago silenced by the English guns, had done little damage.

Cannonballs continued to arrive out of the drifting smoke, bouncing leisurely before tearing bloody holes in the six-deep Highland ranks. They seemed to be traveling so slowly that it would be easy enough to get out of their way, but if you sighted one coming toward you, it would be the last thing you ever saw.

Rory gripped his round wood and leather target tighter. He rested the tip of his sword — the mighty claymore that could split a man in two — on the ground, conserving his strength for the charge he knew was coming. Why had it not come already?

The charge was the great strength of the ragged Highland army — a screaming, lung-bursting surge that swept all before it in an insanity of pounding feet and slashing swords. It had worked before, at Prestonpans and Falkirk, and it was their only hope today.

Rory thought about what to do when the enemy line was reached. The trick was to pick a soldier and run at him. When you got close, the soldier would lunge with the long bayonet on the end of his musket. If you timed it right, you could knock the musket aside with the target on your left arm and bring the claymore down in a sweeping, deadly arc. Swing the sword to left and right and you were in among the redcoats, too close for their awkward bayonets. Then the enemy line would break and the soldiers would flee. After that, it was easy. All you had to do was run as far as you could, killing anyone you caught.

That was how they had always fought. Not this standing helplessly as cannonballs tore the arms and legs off your friends. And Rory had lost a lot of friends. There was Neil struggling for a final breath at the end of an English rope in Carlisle, Callum drowning in his own blood on an English bayonet at Falkirk and Patrick, the Irish volunteer, gazing in surprise at his stomach, ripped open by one of those damned cannonballs not fifteen minutes ago.

When Rory had left his home and his wife, Morag, hugely pregnant, he had been certain of his dream. He didn't want to drag a crop from the reluctant soil only to have it sold for the profit of some already-rich lord in London. He hated that he could be thrown off his ancestral land because the same lord decided that sheep were more profitable than people. He wanted Scotland to be free again. That powerful dream had led him to this cold, windswept moor, with these other ragged dreamers.

Their dream had almost come true. Last year the Highland army had marched in triumph through the streets of Edinburgh. The English had fled and Scotland was theirs. But Prince Charles Edward Stuart had wanted more. Bonnie Prince Charlie had wanted the throne of England, too. And so they had marched south. Far enough to scare the English king from London, but too far for supplies and support. All last winter had been a long, bitter retreat. But the running was over. The fate of Scotland would be decided this rainy afternoon.

Rory pulled his plaid closer around his shoulders and thought of Morag and the news that he was the father of fine twin boys. Angus and Lachlan he would call them. Good strong names. But what would their future hold if Rory's dream died this day?

Morag had a different dream — to begin a new life in the colonies. There, she said, you could be free, far away from kings, Scottish or English. Rory had laughed when she had begged him to go to the New World instead of to battle, but now he wasn't so sure her dream was wrong, especially if they lost today. And lose they would if the charge wasn't ordered soon.

Almost as Rory thought this, the charge began — not on an order from the prince, but spontaneously. The Clan Chattan, to Rory's left, broke and ran — not as frightened cowards toward the safety of the rear, but as enraged men, toward the guns and bayonets of the English.

It was all Rory and the others needed. Leaving the dead and dying, they were off, plaids pulled high out of the way of pumping legs as they leaped the tussocks of heather. At first, the huge claymores were held low and the men ran in silence, saving their breath, but as they cleared the smoke and saw the enemy, the swords were raised for killing and a mighty primeval shout swept along the line.

Grapeshot tore holes in the Highland charge. Disciplined musket volleys rolled along the redcoat lines. Men were falling all around Rory, but he fixed his attention on a tall soldier in front of him. Raising his sword, he readied the target. But the soldier wasn't doing what he was supposed to — he wasn't trying to lunge at Rory. Instead, he was half turned to his right.

Rory had a brief thought that it was going to be easy before recognizing the trap he was falling into. Instead of battling the wild Highlander in front of them, the redcoats were protecting the man on their right. The Scottish targets were useless — the English could stab in under the upraised sword arm of the man attacking their neighbor. Now the unwieldy length of the bayonet was an advantage.

Rory felt the steel blade tear into the flesh of his side and scrape along his ribs. Desperately, he changed the direction of his blow and swung his sword to the right. He saw it dig deeply into the redcoat's neck, splitting him almost to the breastbone, then Rory's strength drained away and he fell into blackness.

Rory woke to feel the gentle rain falling on his up-turned face. He opened his mouth to moisten his parched tongue. He couldn't move his right arm, his side hurt and his plaid was soaked in blood. But how much was from his own wound and how much from the gash in the neck of the dead English soldier who lay across his body, Rory had no way of knowing.

The battle was over — that was obvious from the silence. The Highlanders had lost — that was obvious from the redcoats stalking about among the bodies. The charge had failed. If Charles Stuart were still alive, he would never be king of Scotland. His Highland army lay dead across Culloden Moor.

Rory felt almost relieved that the dream of a free Scotland was gone. Now there was just him and Morag and the twins to think of. Somehow he had to survive and make Morag's dream come true — escape the bitter English repression that was bound to come and raise a strong family in peace in the Americas.

A harsh voice nearby broke into Rory's thoughts. "This un's still livin'. But not for long."

Rory shivered at the musket shot.

"Hell, Geordie," a second voice added. "That one was not going to get up and fight you. Don't waste the musket balls. Use the bayonet, man."

Slowly and painfully, Rory burrowed deeper beneath the body of the dead redcoat. Every move sent shocks of pain down his side, but eventually the man's body almost completely covered his own. Rory's head was buried in the gore of the man's shoulder, his face covered by lank, greasy hair.

I might be lucky, Rory thought. If I live until dark, I might be able to crawl away. If I travel at night and hide during the day, I might get home. If I don't bleed to death.

WALT

September 15, 1860
The woods near Cornwall, Canada West

Walt sat comfortably on the horse's broad back. His loose buckskin jacket and wool pants kept out the late afternoon chill. A musket rested reassuringly across his back, and his powder horn, bag of musket balls and water canteen hung from his belt. Suspended from his saddle were a dozen grouse and three rabbits. It had been a successful hunt and Walt was content.

The low sun filtered through the trees, creating patches of light and dark on the narrow trail. Birds twittered from branches overhead, small creatures scuttled through the fallen leaves and underbrush and the smell of pine filled the air. It was still mild and the winter stock of game was building well. The steady plod of the horse's hooves on the dry earth sent a catchy tune around in Walt's head. It was a song his father, Kenneth, had taught him, a soldier's song from the War of 1812.

As Walt sang, he wondered if he would ever be a soldier. He was fifteen, old enough to fight, and there was talk of war to the south. There had been talk of little else in the past year, since John Brown had invaded Harpers Ferry, Virginia, and tried to incite a slave revolt. But that had not happened, and Brown had been easily captured and hanged. Since then, war had been on everyone's mind. Perhaps even Canada, united now for nearly twenty years and on the verge of attaining Dominion status within the British Empire, might be drawn in.

The words of the song were about a war long before Walt had been born, but the tune was catchy:

> *"A bold fusilier came marching back through Rochester*
> *Off for the wars in the far country,*
> *And he sang as he marched*
> *Through the crowded streets of Rochester,*
> *'Who'll be a soldier with Wellington and me?'*
>
> *Who'll be a soldier? Who'll be a soldier?*
> *Who'll be a soldier with Wellington and me?*
> *And he sang as he marched,*
> *Through the crowded streets of Rochester,*
> *'Who'll be a soldier with Wellington and me?'"*

Walt enjoyed singing, but he only ever did it while no one was listening. People snickered or groaned, but the trees didn't seem to mind. Gaining confidence from the forest's lack of criticism, Walt belted out the next verse at the top of his lungs:

"The King he has ordered new troops onto the continent,
To strike a last blow at the enemy.
And if you would be a soldier,
All in a scarlet uniform,
Take the King's shilling for Wellington and me.

Take the King's shilling! Take the King's shilling!
Take the King's shilling for Wellington and me.
And he sang as he marched,
Through the crowded streets of Rochester,
'Take the King's shilling for — '"

A deer broke cover to Walt's right and leaped across the track. The horse shied, throwing the boy painfully to the ground. Walt landed on his side, damaging neither the musket nor his back, but he was winded. His horse cantered a few steps before turning to gaze curiously at its former passenger.

"I guess he didn't think much of your singing," said a deep voice. Twisting around, Walt sat up and looked at the approaching figure. He was big, both in height and girth, and had skin of the deepest black. He was wearing patched dungarees over a worn, checked shirt, and both seemed stretched to the limit across his shoulders and chest. His dark, curly hair was strongly flecked with white. Despite the man's considerable age, his huge frame took up most of the path and exuded a sense of power. The musket nestled in the crook of his arm looked more like a whittled stick than a weapon.

"That was my supper for a good few days you scared off with your caterwauling," the man continued. The censure in the words was contradicted by the flashing white of a broad smile.

"Sorry, Touss," Walt said, hauling himself to his feet. "I didn't know you were out hunting, too."

"Well, no matter. There's plenty more deer where that one came from," the man went on as he stood beside Walt's horse, stroking its neck. "I see you've had a successful day."

Walt stepped stiffly forward and shook hands with Touss. "I have had my share of luck. Why don't you take a couple of grouse for supper since I scared yours away?"

"I'll do that," Touss replied with a smile, "but not for the deer — for having to listen to your howling. You should post warnings on the trees when you are out in the woods in full voice."

Walt laughed, used to Touss's teasing. He enjoyed his company and often visited Touss's nearby farm or accompanied him on short hunting expeditions.

Since slavery had been abolished in the British Empire almost thirty years before, Canada had become a haven for slaves escaping from their owners to the south. Several worked as farm laborers around Cornwall, and a few owned a bit of land and some stock.

Touss was the last of a small family who had been granted a parcel of land for supporting the British in the American War of Independence more than eighty years before. His parents and two brothers were buried in a tiny cemetery behind the distinctive blue farmhouse, but Touss kept going. He was even something of a local hero. On November 9, 1813, as a boy of thirteen, Touss had run through the woods to warn the British commander of American landings at Cook's Tavern. The warning had no effect on the battle of Crysler's Farm that broke out by accident two days later, but people still remembered Touss's contribution to repelling the American invasion.

Walt took his horse's reins, and he and Touss walked side by side through the trees. He envied Touss his childhood exploits and hoped that war would come now and give him a chance to be a hero.

"Do you think there's going to be a war?" Walt asked.

"Maybe. Enough people seem to want one."

"I hope so."

"And why would you hope that, young Walter McGregor?"

"To free the slaves, of course," Walt answered quickly, expecting Touss to agree. But the big man kept silent and Walt became increasingly uncomfortable. "And for the adventure," he added.

"The adventure?" Touss asked with a half smile. "Too quiet around here for you, is it?"

"Yes, it is too quiet around here," Walt answered, annoyed that Touss was making fun of him. "Nothing ever happens. And everyone else in my family had adventurous lives. Great-grandfather Rory was almost killed fighting the English at Culloden Moor in Scotland. His sons fought on different sides in the American Revolution. My grandfather, Lachlan, had to flee here afterward, and he never spoke to his twin brother, Angus, again. Even my father did something exciting in the War of 1812, but he won't tell me what."

Touss nodded, but remained silent.

"You fought in the War of 1812, too."

"Well, I wouldn't rightly say that I fought. I did a lot of running about in the woods and told some officers what I had seen, but I never fired a musket. The only things I ever shoot are deer — when I get the chance," he said, flashing a smile.

Walt scowled at not being taken seriously.

"But my names fought in a lot of wars," Touss went on hurriedly.

"Your names?"

"Sure. I don't tell many people this, but I'm not merely Touss Washington. My full name is," Touss pulled himself up to his full height and puffed out his chest in mock importance, "Toussaint L'Ouverture Spartacus Prosser Washington."

Touss laughed at the expression of amazement on Walt's face.

"Sure is a mouthful. That's why I just go by Touss. Seems to make people more comfortable."

"Why all those names?"

"Well," Touss explained, "I was born on the first day of the century. My daddy was a freed slave, and he believed with a passion that this new century would see the end of slavery. To prepare me for the golden age of freedom, he gave me the names of famous men who had fought against slavery in the past. Spartacus led a revolt of slaves against the Romans near two thousand years ago, Toussaint L'Ouverture freed the slaves of Santo Domingo, and Gabrielle Prosser led slaves to attack Richmond just four months before I was born. Now, from all that famous collection of heroes, I could find none that wasn't a great trial for people hereabouts to remember, so I shortened the first to Touss and that is how I have been known since Adam was a boy."

"So if you had been born now, you might have been called John Brown?"

"I suppose I might have been," Touss replied with another smile, "or Nat Turner or Denmark Vassey. There are a lot of brave men to choose from."

"Well, I think there will be a war, and I think we will be a part of it. Then I will get *my* chance."

"Don't go looking for war," Touss said, suddenly serious. "If it comes looking for you and you must fight, then fight your hardest for what you believe is right, but war is not a thing to seek out."

"But the people you are named for sought out war."

"They did," Touss said, "but they had few choices. They were slaves. It ain't right for one human being to own another, or to whip, beat or brand a man. Either a slave accepts his lot or he rises up. He can just run away, if he has somewhere to run to, or he can rebel. My namesakes chose rebellion, but they were not some muddleheaded colonial boy wishing to fight in someone else's war.

"Now, enough talk of war. Here is some real singing." Touss cleared his throat and began:

"When the sun comes up and the first quail calls,
Follow the drinking gourd.
For the old man's awaiting to carry you to freedom,
If you follow the drinking gourd.

The riverbank makes a mighty good road.
The dead trees show you the way,
Left foot, peg foot, traveling on
Follow the drinking gourd.

The river ends between two hills.
Follow the drinking gourd.
There's another river on the other side,
Follow the drinking gourd.

Where the great big river meets the little river,
Follow the drinking gourd.
For the old man's awaiting for to carry you to freedom,
If you follow the drinking gourd."

The tuneful melody and Touss's deep, rich voice had Walt humming along. "That's pretty," he said when Touss had finished.

"It's more than pretty. It's an escape map for slaves living in Mississippi and Alabama. And it's a map to use even if you can't read."

"A map?" Walt asked.

"Sure. Midwinter down south, when the quail call, look at the sky and see the Big Dipper. Follow that north to the Tombigbee River, where peg legs carved on the old stumps show the way. Cross the hills to the Tennessee River and keep north to the Ohio River, where someone will meet you and take you to safe houses and Canada. It's all there if you know it. And there are other versions for runaways in other parts of the South."

Walt was amazed that there could be so much in a simple song.

It was almost dark by the time the pair came to a fork in the path. Walt untied a brace of grouse and a rabbit and handed them to Touss.

"Thank you," the big man said, holding up the game. "For a couple of good suppers like this, maybe I'll even let you sing to me again."

Walt laughed. "Be careful, I might just do that."

"Say hello to your father for me," Touss said, turning down the left-hand fork.

"I will," Walt replied, remounting his horse and trotting down the right fork toward home.

NATE

September 15, 1860
McGregor Plantation
Charleston, South Carolina

It was going to be a good crop this year. Nate stood on the low hill, looking out over a sea of white, hundreds of acres of bushes covered in white clumps of cotton. The flowers of May had given way to swelling green bolls that had finally burst, releasing the delicate cotton fibers. Scattered across the fields, scores of black figures moved along the rows, carefully picking the fragile clusters. The slaves' main job was to harvest the cotton before the fall rain could destroy it. Not that rain looked to be a problem this year.

Nate squinted up at the washed-out blue sky. For the sixth straight day, the sun was beating down with malevolent fury. Nate felt the heat as a tangible weight pushing upon him. His wide-brimmed hat provided some shade for his face but no relief, and the sweat trickled down his cheeks and into his already soaking shirt. The hot, dry weather helped with the harvest, but it was affecting people badly. Nate's father, James, was being difficult to live with, finding fault with everything his son did and criticizing the servants harshly. Even the slaves were unsettled, and there had been two runaways in the past week.

Nate turned his gaze back to the fields. He loved this view, not simply because it was scenic, but because he loved cotton. He was in awe of how a simple, unremarkable plant could produce something so remarkable. Cotton clothed the world. True, there was silk for the very rich and wool for the poor, but neither was as practical or as hard-wearing as cotton. Even the worn-out scraps could be reprocessed into paper. Cotton made the world a better place.

But the day was getting late. It was time to head back. With a last lingering look over the busy fields, Nate strolled down the hill to the huddle of plantation sheds and the distant, shimmering white of the plantation house. He approached one of the cotton sheds, a dark, empty cavern awaiting the valuable bales that would be stacked inside in a few days. The darkness looked cool. The sweat-stained boy knew it was an illusion, that the interior would be only a degree or two cooler than outside, but any escape from the merciless sun was inviting.

Inside, Nate stood immobile, waiting for his eyes to adjust to the darkness. That was when he heard the noise to his left, a rustle followed by a grunt of pain.

"Hello?" he said into the darkness. "Is something wrong?" His question was met with silence. "Can I help?" He edged toward the sound, holding his hand out in front of him. The darkness was thinning as his eyes adjusted, and Nate could see the vague outlines of equipment, but the shadows were still impenetrable. "I won't hurt you," Nate said as he worked his way forward.

All of a sudden, a figure exploded from the deep shadows, cannoning into Nate and knocking him, breathless, on his back. Nate's hands scrabbled to get a grip on his attacker, but he wasn't fast enough. Digging a knee into Nate's stomach, his assailant was on his feet and out the door into the light while Nate lay gasping for breath. All Nate saw was a black back streaked with red.

Pulling himself painfully to his feet, Nate stumbled to lean against the doorjamb. The ground in front of the shed was empty. Shaking his head in frustration, Nate went to dust off his clothes, but his right hand, the one that had grabbed at the intruder, was covered in blood.

"Best wash that off. There's no telling what diseases you might catch from slave blood." A man slouched casually against the corner of the shed, incongruously dressed in a long-tailed coat, a misshapen black hat and a red waistcoat more suited to a riverboat gambler than a plantation manager. As always, he carried a brown whip coiled over his left shoulder.

Frank King's face was narrow, and his eyes were continually on the move. Nate hated the way King never looked directly at him — there was a slyness to it. King spoke politely enough when Nate's father was around, but even then, there was an insolence to his tone.

"Do you know anything about this?" Nate asked.

"I might," King replied with a sneer, "but it ain't nothing you need trouble yourself about."

"It might be something my father needs to trouble himself about. That man has been whipped."

King spat into the dust in front of Nate. "Daresay he deserved it," he said. "Only way to deal with troublemakin' blacks, I reckon."

"Was it you whipped him?"

"Maybe, but no matter."

"It does matter." Nate felt his anger rising. "Don't forget who owns this plantation."

"And don't forget who runs it," King shot back. "You need me. Without slaves you're nothing, and who keeps them slaves in line? Me. That's who. I keep them doing what you and your father want. It's me and my whip keeps you from feeling your belly twist with hunger and lurch with fear. Without me you'd be murdered in your beds. Slaves need discipline."

Nate felt his anger turn to frustration. He knew there was some truth to what King said. "Discipline, yes, but not cruelty."

"Cruelty!" King's sneer was replaced by a scowl. "What do you know of cruelty, you self-righteous pup? You live a grand life in the big house, attended to on every hand. I'll tell you about cruelty.

"Cruelty is a small boy in a dirt-poor sod house on a scratch farm outside Jerusalem, Somerset County, Virginia. It's that boy hiding in a pile of linens while someone batters down the door. It's that boy watching black men swarm in and slaughter his brother and father before they can defend themselves. It's that boy hearing his mother scream as she has her head caved in and smelling the blood when his baby sister was hurled on the hearth."

"You!"

"Yes, me. Twenty-nine years since Nat Turner's killing spree. Slave revolt! Murder's more like it. But we paid them back all right. Weren't no blacks safe from our boys riding through the county like avenging angels, hanging, burning and shooting until there weren't one of those murdering savages left. I was with them and I would do it again, and more. So don't talk to me about cruelty."

Nate shivered at the horror of King's outburst. Had that really happened?

As he watched, the anger drained from King's face and the sneer returned. "But soon you'll have to get yourself someone else to keep you safe. There's a better living to be made catching runaways. Owners are paying good money for returned slaves, whatever their condition. And there's a war coming. No telling what opportunities that might present."

Nate could think of nothing to say. He was overwhelmed by the rage in the man before him. With all the dignity he could muster, he turned and headed toward the house.

"I shall be the best of them bounty hunters," King shouted after him, "because I never give up! Your father may have use of me again, one day."

Nate hated Frank King — that was easy. But even King couldn't have deserved the things he said had happened to him. Perhaps every time he beat a slave on the McGregor plantation, he was avenging his family. Could such brutality be justice?

Nate was confused for another reason. In the instant he had seen the slave outside the shed, he had recognized him — Sunday, only a year or two older than Nate. They had spent many happy hours playing in the dirt and the woods around the plantation.

Nate had assumed that their friendship would last forever. But it didn't. One day, his father pulled him aside and told him very firmly that he was becoming a young man now and that it was beneath his station to play with a Negro boy.

Nate had been distraught, but James had been adamant. "You are growing up — and into your place in the world," he had said. "You have a station, as does Sunday, and they are not the same."

For days, Nate had moped around the house hating everyone. But his adjustment had been helped by Sunday's increasing bitterness and, later, by his attempts to escape.

Nate was at the old plantation house now. He looked up at the wide steps with the tall grecian pillars fronting the deep porch. It always made him feel as if he were entering a gaping mouth. The entrance had scared him as a small child, but now it was welcoming, drawing him into the cool, echoing hallway that was the heart of the house. Sometimes, when important people came to visit and he had to be on his best behavior, the scale and formality of the hall made him feel uncomfortable, but mostly he loved it. He stood there now, breathing in great gulps of cool air.

In front of him, the oak staircase rose to a landing, where it split into two, curving to either side of a wide, sweeping hall, off which the many bedrooms lay.

To Nate's left was the formal dining room, little used these days. Behind that was a breakfast room and, along a narrow corridor beside the stairs, the kitchens and stairs to the attic. To Nate's right, behind two heavy sliding doors, was his father's office. It had once been the social center of the house, a large, sumptuous parlor where guests conversed, danced and sang around the grand piano. With no desire to entertain since his wife's death, James McGregor had turned the room into an office, lining the walls with bookshelves and placing a large desk and chair to one side of the wide fireplace.

Nate loved that fireplace. It was huge and intricately carved from shining white marble. When he gazed hard into the cool stone, he could see the tiny fossilized fragments that had lived in some vanished ocean.

The fireplace was also a link to the family's past.

As the McGregors had prospered, the house had been much added to and enhanced, but the fireplace was original. Rory McGregor had built his wife, Morag, and the twins a modest house around a palatial fireplace — their own fireplace — as if, even in the humidity and heat of South Carolina, he was still fighting off the gnawing cold of the Scottish Highlands.

That fireplace had seen the twins grow into men and, on a January day in 1784, had silently watched as they said good-bye forever. There had been many reasons for that good-bye — disagreements about the future of the plantation, Angus's support of the American revolutionaries in the war just ended and those revolutionaries' unforgiving attitude to Lachlan, who had supported the British — but the main gulf was slavery.

Angus wanted to change the crop from indigo to cotton. He believed, as did many other plantation owners, that it was the crop of the future. Angus was even engaged to marry Miss Jane Heyward, a daughter of one of the most respected families and largest cotton growers in the state. With the support of her family, the success of the plantation was assured. There was only one drawback. To grow cotton economically, you needed slaves.

To Angus's way of thinking, their father, Rory, had fled Scotland to save his family from the crushing poverty enforced by the English landlords — to give his sons the chance to better themselves. They were on the verge of that prosperity now, and a few black slaves should not stand in the way of fulfilling Rory's dream.

Lachlan agreed that their father had fled Scotland to escape servitude. But he was adamant that, to enslave others, even blacks, was to betray Rory's dream of freedom.

So the bitter good-bye had been said in front of that fireplace, and Lachlan had gone north to the British colonies.

Nate wondered as he stood in the hall what unknown relatives he had at the other end of the continent. Nate missed having a family. There was only himself and his father. He loved his father, but James McGregor was old — and acted that way. Right now, he would be sitting at the desk by the fireplace working on the plantation accounts that seemed to take up all his time these days. Nate decided not to interrupt him to complain about King. He had calmed down a bit and, given his father's mood of late, he would just tell Nate to keep out of the overseer's business. Nate shrugged and headed back to the kitchen to see if there was a cool drink to be had.

SUNDAY

September 23, 1860
Banks of the Santee River, South Carolina

Sunday was the only name he had, unless you counted the plantation owner's family name, and he wanted no part of that. Sunday would do — it was the Lord's day and the day he was born. Perhaps it would be the day he died, because on this Sunday the hounds were getting close, and he had sworn never to be taken alive. This time he would get to the promised land for sure — the one in this world or the one in the next.

Sunday and Joshua had been on the run for a week, traveling at night and lying up by the riverbank during the day. The marks of Sunday's last whipping had almost healed, but they still pained enough that he slept on his stomach. That was something else Sunday swore would never happen again. No man would whip him — or brand him.

Sunday shuddered at the memory of the pain — and the smell — when his owner's initials had been seared into his shoulder with a red hot iron. That had been after his first escape. He had been whipped that time, too, and the second, and the third.

The third had been the worst. Frank King had become overseer then, and Sunday would never forget the man's smile as he laid on the whip. It had twisted something inside Sunday. He had called King the most terrible things he could think of, some he didn't even know he knew. King had laughed and called other men over to hold Sunday down. Then King took his knife, pulled out Sunday's tongue and cut it off.

The horror of the blade slicing through his tongue still made Sunday shiver. He had almost died then, but something hard as diamond had formed instead — part hatred of King and part a promise to escape again and, if he was caught, to die rather than be taken back.

The hardness also made Sunday unforgiving. Not everyone on the plantation had been as cruel as Frank King, but Sunday had to hate them as well. Nate, the plantation owner's son, had always been kind to Sunday. He had found Sunday after his tongue was mutilated, taken him to his own house and sent for the doctor to tend him. Nate and Sunday had been friends as children, but Nate would always be white and Sunday black. Sunday had drawn into himself and nursed the hardness at the core of his being.

He had even turned against his family. Sunday's father was a gentle man who accepted the world the way it was. For him, slavery was something to be endured — not good, but the way God had organized things and therefore to be suffered in silence. Sunday couldn't believe that — meek acceptance was as intolerable as King's viciousness. It was only Sunday's hardness that kept him alive.

The still-raw whipping of eight days ago was by no means his worst — King hadn't even told him why he was being punished. What had terrified Sunday had been the possibility that King had heard of his and Joshua's plan to escape. But they had gone ahead anyway, and the plan had worked.

The pair were a long way from the plantation now, but they had even longer to go. If they followed the rivers like the song said, they would eventually get to a place where people would help them, but they still wouldn't be safe. Even where there were no slaves, a runaway was property and could be captured and returned to his owner. The only safe place was Canada — the promised land. Sunday looked up. Through a gap in the trees, he could see the familiar shape of the drinking gourd, the handle curved like a finger, beckoning him.

A hound bayed frighteningly close — bounty hunters. Tapping Joshua on the shoulder, Sunday pointed to the swirling waters of the river and made swimming motions. Joshua nodded. The pair crawled down the bank and slipped into the cold water. Part swimming, part hauling along on exposed tree roots, the pair dragged themselves toward freedom.

WALT

November 18, 1860
McGregor Farm
Cornwall, Canada West

Walt moved the bucket of milk aside and leaned on the stall rail.

"Well, McKenzie," he said, "maybe we didn't go to war a year ago over John Brown, but it looks like we might now over this Lincoln fellow."

The byre was one of Walt's favorite haunts, especially in winter. It was small, so it stayed warm, and Walt often lingered after the milking so that he could enjoy the rich odors of the piled hay bales and of McKenzie herself. She was his to milk, feed, care for and talk to. There were few boys Walt's age on the farms nearby, so McKenzie provided welcome companionship. She wasn't much of a conversationalist, but she never argued, and Walt found her shuffling and chewing noises comforting. This evening, he had a lot on his mind.

"This man Lincoln, who nobody's ever heard of, is to be the American president, and the Southern states have vowed to break away from the union — secession it's called. Lincoln has said he will fight to preserve the union, so that means war. Touss says that, whatever the politicians say, it will be a war about slavery. This is good. If the northern states can destroy that evil institution, that would be worth fighting for."

McKenzie tilted her head and gazed at Walt with her large, watery eyes.

"You know, McKenzie, sometimes I yearn for a simple life like yours — no worries except where the next mouthful of hay is coming from." The cow blinked slowly. Walt leaned over and gently stroked the beast's long nose.

"You don't have to worry about war, do you?"

As if in answer, McKenzie sneezed, covering Walt's arm and side in warm wetness. "McKenzie!" he said. "You really can be disgusting." He wiped the worst of the mess off. "I am not going to tell you any more about the big, wide world unless you behave. Anyway, I have to go now. It's my turn to cook dinner."

McKenzie shook her head and resumed chewing contemplatively. Walt lifted the bucket of milk, stepped outside and pulled the door to. He whistled off-key as he strolled toward the house, where his father sat on the front step smoking a long curved pipe and enjoying the unusually mild evening. As Walt approached, Kenneth, in a deep, rich voice, added words to the tune.

"Ye sons of Anacreon, then, join Hand in Hand;
Preserve Unanimity, Friendship and Love!
'Tis yours to support what's so happily plann'd;
You've the Sanctions of Gods, and the Fiat of Jove.
While thus we agree, Our Toast let it be
May our club flourish happy, united and free!
And long may the Sons of Anacreon intwine
The myrtle of Venus with Bacchus's Vine."

By the time the last words had died away, Walt had joined his father on the porch. He put the milk bucket down and sat on the top step.

"Now that's a fine old song," Kenneth observed.

"I know," Walt said. "You taught it to me — you only ever teach me old songs."

Kenneth laughed. "Perhaps I do, but this one appears to be becoming popular with our American neighbors. I should say, the tune is. They have written new words, all about glaring rockets and gleaming twilights. I must endeavor to learn them. But how is McKenzie?"

"Very well," Walt replied, "although she sneezed on me."

Kenneth chuckled. "That is a cow's nature."

"I was telling her about the coming war."

"Ah, yes." Kenneth took a long draw on his pipe. "A fearful number of people certainly seem to want one."

"Do you think Canada will be drawn in?" Walt asked.

"It's possible. A lot of madmen crawl out of the woodwork when the drums begin a-beating."

"But not all wars are fought by madmen."

"True enough," Kenneth agreed. "But perhaps the idea of war makes sane men a bit mad."

"Our ancestors weren't mad and they fought in wars," Walt said.

"I hope they weren't — although it might explain my son's conversations with cows."

"Or your singing of old songs with words that no one understands," Walt responded.

"Touché. It is always difficult to be sure why people did things years ago. I am sure, though, that their decisions were just as complex as ours."

"But great-grandfather Rory's decision was simple — he went to fight the English."

"The very English who are all that stand between us and our expanding Southern neighbor. And remember, Rory went to war when his wife was pregnant with twins. I doubt if that was a simple decision. Then there were his sons — your grandfather, Lachlan, fought for the English against the American revolutionaries his twin brother, Angus, supported."

"Why did the brothers part?" Walt asked.

"Well, Lachlan never talked much about the family split, but I believe it was mostly over the owning of slaves."

"Angus owned slaves?"

"Or wanted to, at least. But that wasn't unusual. Slavery was still legal in the British Empire in those days. What was unusual was Lachlan's refusal to have slaves."

Walt pondered what his father was saying. "Do we have relatives down where Angus lived?"

"Almost certainly. Your great-uncle Angus was on the verge of becoming a respectable member of the southern gentry. You probably have rich slave-owning cousins somewhere in South Carolina."

"They might really own slaves?"

"Probably." Kenneth fiddled with his pipe. "I believe Angus was going into cotton, and you can't grow cotton without slaves."

"But slavery's evil."

"Probably not to the slave owner."

"How can anyone think it isn't evil?" Walt asked indignantly. "Touss says slaves are whipped and branded."

Kenneth tapped the ash out of his pipe bowl and leaned back on the steps. "I agree with you and Touss that slavery is evil. But I also recognize that we are in the minority in thinking that —"

"We can't be," Walt interrupted. "We don't have slavery here."

"True, but then we don't have the climate to grow cotton."

Kenneth held up his hand to stave off his son's indignant denial. "Be that as it may, only the other day,

I read in the paper about a man who was tarred, feathered and run out of town merely for suggesting that black men were as intelligent as white men. A black man doesn't have much chance to advance himself, even in this free land of plenty.

"I reckon a slave owner in South Carolina would claim that a slave is better off than a free black man working in a factory in the north, living in a slum and having his family die of consumption."

Walt frowned with concentration. His father was just making it complicated.

"But what about branding?" Walt argued, latching on to the most horrific aspect he could think of.

"Branding is inhuman, yes. But even that can be said to be in a slave's interest."

"How?"

For a long moment, Kenneth busied himself refilling and lighting his pipe. "Well," he said eventually, "if a slave escapes, he is most likely going to be captured by a bounty hunter who will sell him for a profit. Bounty hunters are brutal men from what I hear, and they care little if a slave or two dies or what condition a slave is in when sold. There are plenty of poor farmers who will buy a slave cheap and not ask too many questions. If a slave is branded, the bounty hunter knows who owns the slave. He also knows he will not be paid if the owner's property isn't returned in reasonable condition. So a captured runaway is treated better if he is branded."

"That's horrible!" Walt exclaimed.

Kenneth nodded. "We branded McKenzie."

"But that's so that we would recognize her ..." Walt's voice trailed off as he realized the trap. "But people aren't cattle."

"Some folk think they are. But even so, I'm told most slaves are well cared for and well fed — like McKenzie. And think of this — cotton has to be picked by hand. If the plantation owners had to pay wages, the price of cotton would increase. Clothes would be expensive and that would cause great hardship amongst the poor. Even paper made from old rags would increase in price. It would cost more to write a letter or buy a shirt. If there was no such thing as slavery, many poor people would suffer."

"It's too complicated!" Walt exclaimed in frustration.

"It certainly is," Kenneth agreed. "That's why I love our little farm. This is about as simple as life gets. Enjoy it, but don't assume everyone thinks your way."

"That's why I like talking to McKenzie," Walt said. "She listens but doesn't complicate everything I say."

Kenneth laughed. "And a good thing, too. The last thing we need is a cow's point of view.

"Now, slavery or not, you put that milk in the cold cellar and get our supper on the stove or we will go to bed hungry tonight."

December 20, 1860
Charleston, South Carolina

Arms and legs flapping crazily, the limp body in the dark clothes and black stovepipe hat flew through the air and landed in a cloud of sparks on the bonfire. The crowd cheered as the flames engulfed the straw-filled form.

"That's how we'll treat all Northern abolitionists!" a wild-eyed man yelled. The crowd's cheering redoubled.

Nate wandered about town while his father conducted business in their hotel suite. He turned away from the bonfire toward St. Andrew's Hall. All around him, the mass of people ebbed and flowed with no apparent purpose. Most were shouting or singing and waving placards denouncing Lincoln or celebrating independence. The flickering light of the many bonfires in the street and the dark shadows of the people dancing around them made Nate think of preachers' tales of the Devil tormenting the damned in hell. The ringing church bells did nothing to reassure him.

Outside St. Andrew's Hall, things were quieter. Knots of people stood around the wide steps talking quietly. Nate caught snippets of conversation.

"It means war!"

"Never! The North has not the will to fight."

"The other Southern states will join us within the week."

"This is the birth of a great new nation."

One man in particular seemed to be attracting attention. He was short, but powerfully built and with a deep, resonant voice. But what he was saying did not seem to be popular.

"It is insanity," he said. "We are rushing to break the Union apart without a thought for what will happen. If there is a war, we will be standing amidst ruins in a year or two. Even if there isn't, South Carolina will never manage on her own."

"By damn, she will!" a red-faced man shouted. "She has a great history and will have a great future."

"Great she may be," the first man replied, "but she is the wrong size — too small to be an independent nation and too large for an insane asylum."

Nate thought the second man was going to strike the speaker, but both were distracted by the appearance of a figure on the hall steps, waving a piece of paper.

"I have in my hand," he roared, "a document signed by one hundred and sixty-nine good men and true. They are your representatives, and they have come together at this historic moment to determine our course." The crowd had fallen silent and was listening expectantly.

"They were unanimous in accepting this document. I shall read what it says." The man fumbled with the paper and squinted in the poor light. "We, the people of the State of South Carolina, in Convention assembled, do hereby declare and ordain ... that the union now subsisting between South Carolina and other States, under the name of 'The United States of America,' is hereby dissolved."

The man continued to speak, but his words were swamped by cheering. Dissolved! The word sped down the street with a life of its own — dissolved, dissolved, the Union is dissolved. Soon, it seemed to Nate, the entire city was shouting the word.

Swept up in this outpouring of joyful emotion, Nate felt powerful, ready to march off and do battle for this new nation whose birth he was witnessing. That one word — dissolved — scratched on a piece of paper had the power to change the world. South Carolina was now a nation.

Turning to rush back to the hotel and share the heady moment with his father, Nate found himself face to face with the man who had been spreading gloom.

"Enjoy the moment, boy," the man said. "There will not be many more of them. I fear there are battlefields calling you and your kind."

Nate wanted to tell the man he was wrong. There would be no battlefields, and even if there were, they would be glorious. Couldn't he see that? But the man had vanished into the crowd.

SUNDAY

December 25, 1860
Adirondack Mountains near Plattsburgh, New York

Sunday shivered and pulled his coat tighter around his shoulders. It was a good coat. Without it, he would have frozen to death for sure. Sunday smiled remembering the man in Wilmington who had given the coat to him. "You'll be needing this if you're to cross the mountains in winter," he had said. And he had been right. Joshua was suffering greatly in his threadbare jacket and scarf. But things had gone well.

It was over three months since their escape. The journey was taking longer than Sunday had imagined, but others had told him he was lucky — it sometimes took more than a year to get as far as they were now. If the weather held, it would be just a few days more — over the mountains and across the river to the promised land.

Through the trees to the north, Sunday could see the drinking gourd twinkling coldly. It had been his companion since the escape — as he listened to the hounds on the Santee, as he searched for the porch lights of safe houses in Pennsylvania and as he struggled along wilderness trails in the mountains. It was an old friend now.

Sunday's memories of the last weeks were a patchwork of alternating fear and relief in which occasional incidents stood out starkly. There was the panic of the first few days, running until his lungs hurt, traveling at night and lying up in bramble thickets in daylight, terrified by every distant dog barking. There was the night Joshua had collapsed with the fever and Sunday had taken a chance on a house with a lantern in the window. They'd been lucky. The Quaker family had taken them in and nursed Joshua back to health. Then there had been the guides, rushed and harried men who had passed them on in the dead of night to the next safe house — all the way to Wilmington.

Sunday had been amazed by Wilmington, the first city he had seen close up. It seemed a huge, confusing mass of people, horses, carriages and buildings. How could there be so many people in the world? The most Sunday had ever seen had been the few hundred on the plantation. Now he was swimming amongst countless thousands, all busily going about tasks Sunday could only guess at.

As Delaware was a free state, Wilmington was also the first place the pair had been able to show themselves in daylight. They still had to be careful — there were bounty hunters everywhere — but they could take short excursions in the city. The wonders of Wilmington had been followed by the vastness of Philadelphia and New York.

During the last two weeks, Sunday, Joshua and four other escapees had hurriedly worked their way up the Hudson River to Plattsburgh on Lake Champlain. If they were to make it over the mountains before the snow became too deep, time was important. So far, things had gone well. It was cold, colder than Sunday could ever have imagined, but the snow had held off for this final leg of the journey.

Sunday drew his gaze away from the friendly stars and looked about him. The six escapees were huddled around a large fire in what clothes or blankets they had. The others, including Joshua, were already asleep. Only the guide sat awake on the far side of the blaze.

The fire crackled loudly, throwing sparks up into the night and casting wild shadows on the surrounding trees. Sunday turned now to warm his back. And that was why he didn't see the dark shadows creeping from the trees on the far side of the fire.

He first heard the guide's muffled shout. As he turned, a musket butt swept past him, catching his forehead. Dazed, Sunday fell sideways as chaos erupted around him. He saw a figure standing over him, musket above his head. As the musket descended, Sunday raised

his arms to protect his head. There was no need —
before the blow fell, the attacker was swept aside by
Joshua's flying body.

Sunday struggled to his feet. The air was filled
with shouts, screams and curses. The man who had
attacked Sunday was locked in a struggle with Joshua.
Sunday went to help his friend. Together, the
runaways wrestled the musket free. Joshua held it
uncertainly as their attacker stepped back between
them and the fire.

A glint of steel in the firelight warned Sunday of
the pistol in the man's hand just as a deafening
explosion echoed around the clearing. Joshua staggered
backward, the musket slipping from his hand. Sunday
grabbed his friend, who was plucking ineffectually at a
ragged red hole in his chest. Then Joshua went limp,
dragging Sunday down with him.

Sunday gazed at his dying friend — they had come
so far together. Overwhelmed by rage, he grabbed the
fallen musket, swung it upward and pulled the trigger.
He didn't know if the gun was cocked or even loaded.
It was both.

Sunday's ears rang from the noise, and his shoulder
ached from the kicking musket. Joshua's murderer flew
backward and landed amid a shower of sparks in the
heart of the fire.

For a moment, everything was still. Then, as the
heat set his clothing and hair alight, the man screamed,
an unearthly, high-pitched sound. Across the fire, a man
was shouting and pointing. "That one shot Jesse!"

Sunday froze, a chill of horror slipping down his spine. A moment before, he had been looking to the future and freedom. Now he could see only the past. It had followed him, wouldn't let him escape. It would stop at nothing to prevent him going to the promised land. Across the fire stood Frank King.

Sunday hurled the musket away and fled into the trees. A musket ball crashed into a trunk above his head, but he was soon enveloped by darkness. The last thing he heard was Frank King's voice raised above Jesse's weakening screams. "I'll get you! I swear, if it's the last thing I do, I'll see you hang."

N A T E

Midnight, December 31, 1860
McGregor Plantation
Charleston, South Carolina

Nate knocked and, without waiting for a reply, slid open the heavy doors of his father's study. A low fire burned fitfully in the large grate. Even though it was late on the last day of the year, his father sat at the desk, a pile of papers in front of him. Deep lines of worry creased his forehead.

"Is everything all right?" Nate asked.

"What?" His father looked up from his deep reverie. "All right? Yes. Yes. Just accounts. Nothing that need concern you."

James McGregor pushed his chair back noisily and stood. He was a tall, distinguished man. His face was wrinkled with age, but his eyes were bright and alert. Above them, a mop of snow-white hair completed the picture of a man confident in his abilities and of his place in God's grand scheme of things.

"Let us sit by the fire," he said, gesturing toward the high-backed chairs on either side of the hearth. As he slid around the desk, James's long-fingered, almost delicate hand found a cut-crystal glass on the red leather surface. "I have taken the liberty of procuring you a good measure of cold lemonade so that we need not be disturbed by the servants."

James passed the glass over to his son. Reaching back, he collected an identical glass half full of amber liquid. Holding his glass up to the firelight, James studied it contemplatively. "If there is one thing I have inherited from Angus and Rory," he said, "it is an appreciation for fine malt scotch whiskey. The bourbon they drink hereabouts cannot compare.

"A toast." James raised his glass to Nate and intoned the wish Nate had heard many times before. "May those who live truly be always believed, and those who deceive be always deceived."

Father and son sipped their drinks. The boy was almost as tall as his father, with a wiry strength missing in the old man and a shock of red instead of white hair.

"Well," James said as the pair sat, "here we are in a new nation on the verge of a new year."

Nate nodded absently. The new year certainly promised excitement, but Nate had been dwelling on the year just past. It had been tumultuous, even on the plantation — an unprecedented number of runaways.

And Frank King had left to go bounty hunting. Nate's mind drifted back to the afternoon when he had been bowled over by Sunday running out of the shed. Over the following days, Nate had visited the slave town looking for his friend, but there had been no sign of him. Sunday had run.

"What are you thinking on, Son?"

"Oh," Nate replied, "that mute slave, Sunday."

"You must put him from your mind, Nathaniel," his father responded, surprisingly angry. "He is lost to us in the iniquitous dens of New York or amongst the abolitionists. You must not become overly attached to slaves. Treat them as well as they deserve, but never forget that they are slaves and are not ... reliable.

"They are not like us. They have been only recently brought from savagery and are closer to the primitive, without our generations of culture and upbringing. Individually, they may be fine specimens, but it will be many generations, if ever, before they can be raised up to the level of the white man. The savage in them is strong. Even half-breeds lapse back into the primitive. Look what happened down in Santo Domingo. That Toussaint L'Ouverture — they slaughtered near sixty thousand people. Men, women and children butchered in their beds."

Nate sat back, surprised at the vehemence in his father's voice. He was trying to think of some response when James continued. "And now these Northerners have forced us to secede. It is hard enough making a profit these days without that."

"Will it mean war?" Nate asked.

"Who can say? The Constitution does not allow the North to take up arms against us, but I cannot trust that man Lincoln and those Unionist hotheads in Washington."

"If it comes to war, I will fight." Nate gestured wildly, but spoiled the effect of his grand pronouncement by spilling half his lemonade on the hearth.

His father smiled. "I believe you will — and even that you should, if it comes to that," he said. "But let us hope you do not have to. Let us drink to good news in the coming months."

As Nate leaned over to clink glasses, he was surprised to see what looked like a tear glint in his father's eye.

heels in love with the young, flighty and romantic Emma. She had been attracted to the rough farmer, and when he proposed, she had accepted. But she was a city girl, unsuited to the hard life of a farm. She yearned for the city's intellectual and social whirl, and even Walt's birth in 1845 hadn't strengthened her ties to country life. Eventually, Kenneth had let her go, and Emma returned to Montreal.

Emma was a poet and story writer and had even been published in the *Literary Garland* magazine. Walt had tried to read a few of her stories but found them a chore. They were clever, but not much happened in them. Walt preferred *The Leatherstocking Tales* and the adventures of Natty Bumpo. Still, his mother had met the literary lights of her day and knew Susanna Moodie. Emma needed the literary life as much as Kenneth had to have the farm.

Walt found himself oddly happy in both their worlds. He loved the farm and the hard work, looking after the stock and the fields, and he would die without the endless wilderness in which to hunt and roam. But he loved the city, too, the noise and bustle and the exciting new ideas that Emma's friends talked about.

"So, Father, when can we set out?"

Kenneth smiled at his son's enthusiasm. "As soon as the weather improves, and —"

"What was that?" Walt tilted his head to the side.

"What was what? I didn't hear anything."

"I thought I heard a knocking." Walt turned to face the door to the kitchen.

WALT

Midnight, December 31, 1860
McGregor Farm
Cornwall, Canada West

"Here's to the new year. May it be quieter than everyone expects." At sixty-three, Kenneth McGregor exuded strength. He was not tall, but broad and muscular. His hair still retained its color, if severely thinned on top. His face was dark and leathery from long hours outdoors, but the blue eyes still gleamed, and he could outwork many a younger man in the fields.

Kenneth raised his tumbler, one-quarter full of rough whiskey, in a toast to his son. Walt's glass had only a splash in it, but it burned his throat, making him cough and splutter.

"You're almost sixteen. It's time you learned to drink whiskey," his father said with a laugh. "You'll have to if you're to be a McGregor. If you don't, old

Rory's ghost will haunt you. He was a great one for the whiskey, by all accounts."

"I'll try," Walt gasped in reply. He had yet to fill out into his full muscular bulk, but he was already strong. He would be good-looking one day, once the wispy fluff on his upper lip thickened into a decent mustache or was shaved off. Walt had his mother's sad eyes, but the rest of him was McGregor, from the large feet to the shock of red hair that refused to be tamed.

The pair sat themselves in the armchairs on either side of the roaring parlor fire. Outside, the icy wind rattled the eaves and blew curtains of snow from New York State over the frozen St. Lawrence River.

"The papers say there will be war this year," Walt said.

"Perhaps," Kenneth replied quietly, looking over at his son. "Let us hope they are wrong. But I wouldn't bet the farm on it. No one is working very hard to avoid war as far as I can see. This man Lincoln seems to be digging in his heels, and that will just enrage the hothead secessionists in the South. I hope we can stay out of it."

"How can we be drawn in?" Walt asked. "It's not our fight. What's it to us if states secede?"

"Nothing, indeed, but I think Touss might be right — even if the war begins over secession, it will soon be about slavery. If the war is long — and I cannot see it being otherwise — slavery will become the cause to fight for or against, and slavery is a very emotional issue."

"At least we'll be fighting in a good cause."

"Maybe," Kenneth said. "But many important people in the North regard our country as simply a state that has not yet got around to joining the Union. They may try to use this war to force us to do that. Then we would fight with the South."

"We would fight *for* slavery?" Walt asked incredulously.

"No." Kenneth was adamant. "We would not be fighting to protect slavery but to keep our freedom. Someone else fighting the Union for their own reasons may help us, but it does not mean we are fighting for the same thing."

"You're making it all so complicated again," Walt sighed helplessly.

"Not me," his father said. "The world is a complex place. But enough talk of war. Let us look forward hopefully. What say we make a visit to the city? We can say hello to your mother, and there will be entertainments aplenty."

"Could we?" Walt asked excitedly. He loved their trips to Montreal and his mother's very different world. Walt saw his mother only once every year or two, as Emma and Kenneth McGregor had lived apart since Walt was five years old.

Emma was Kenneth's second wife. His first, Margaret, had helped him build the farm but had died in the cholera epidemic of 1834. Lonely after Margaret's death, Kenneth had made an extended to Montreal. There, he had met and fallen head

"It's just the wind," Kenneth said. "It's a foul night. But, about Montreal. Let's —"

"There it is again. I'm going to check."

"I didn't hear anything, but go if you must. Just don't let too much cold air in."

Walt rose, placed his whiskey glass by his chair and went through to the kitchen. The fire in the range had burned low, and the kitchen was cold. Walt was halfway across the room when he heard the noise a third time. It was soft but unmistakable — someone was knocking on the back door.

Walt hesitated. Who was it? Should he call his father? What if it was outlaws from across the river? Walt shrugged. Outlaws wouldn't knock softly, and anyway, they probably had more sense than to be out in such a storm. Anyone out on this night probably needed help. Walt opened the door.

A blast of cold wind, a flurry of snow and a ragged shape exploded into the kitchen. Walt jumped back as the figure collapsed in a heap. Beneath the snow and ice, he could see that it was a man, black and wearing a motley assortment of clothing and scarves, but bareheaded and gloveless.

"What's going on?" Kenneth came into the kitchen. "Good God, who's this?" He crouched by the fallen man's head. "There's no need for us all to freeze," he instructed Walt. "Close the door."

Walt had to move the stranger's legs to do so and saw that he had no socks and wore only flimsy street shoes.

"He's still breathing. Grab his feet, Walt, we'll take him through to the parlor."

The two half dragged, half carried the unconscious visitor and sat him in Walt's chair by the fire. The man groaned occasionally as the warmth revived him. Snow melted into puddles on the carpet around his feet. Kenneth put Walt's whiskey glass to the man's lips. He sipped and then coughed repeatedly.

"My God!" Walt exclaimed in horror. "He has no tongue."

Three days after their unexpected visitor had burst upon them, Walt sat at the rough table in the kitchen nursing a mug of hot cocoa. The storm was over and the pale winter sun glinted off the fresh snow.

"His name is Sunday."

Touss's huge frame filled the doorway to the storage room, now a sick room.

"How do you know?"

Touss smiled. "Someone cut his tongue out for sure, and his fingers are frostbitten, but he can still hold a pen."

Walt opened his mouth to say something and then closed it abruptly.

"You assumed that a black man couldn't write."

"I mean … that is …," Walt stammered as his face reddened.

"No matter." Touss held up his hand. "Most times you'd be right. Slaves don't get much chance for book learning. Anyways, Sunday can't write much — his name, the alphabet, a few words. He can't tell us where he's from or what happened to him. He's tough though. Not many would have made it alive through that blizzard."

"How's he doing?" Walt asked.

"Pretty good considering as he walked across the river, and who knows how far before that. He'll maybe lose a toe or two, but he's lucky he had that coat — and found your door. I guess colors are tough to see in a snowstorm."

"Colors?" Walt asked.

Touss flashed a smile. "Do you remember singing in the woods awhile back?" Walt nodded. "Do you also recollect that I showed you how a good song should be sung? Well, there's a couple more verses." Keeping the smile on his face, Touss sang softly:

"Cross over the mountains 'fore the big snow falls,
Follow the drinking gourd.
Frozen river makes a mighty good road,
If you follow the drinking gourd.

Blue house shows you the cracklin' fire,
Warms your body and soul.
Freedom's land, ain't never goin' back,
If you follow the drinking gourd."

Realization dawned slowly in Walt's eyes. "The blue house," he said. "Your house. The song leads to it."

Touss broke into laughter. "You look like a shot rabbit, young Walt. You mean to tell me that all these years you never wondered about all the comings and goings at my place?"

"No. I mean, yes. I wondered, but I thought —"

"You thought, because it was just black folks, it wasn't important?"

Walt dropped his eyes in embarrassment. That was exactly what he had thought.

"Don't worry," Touss went on. "The less people think about my blue house, the more it suits me."

"So," Walt said slowly, "Sunday was headed for your place when he stumbled in our door?"

"Yes," Touss replied. "I've been expecting a guide and a party of runaways for some days now. I think Sunday must be one of them, but I don't know what happened to the rest. They might have turned back or been split up in the blizzard. Or they might have been captured. More bounty hunters every month. Sunday is very lucky. With some rest and good food, he should be much improved in a few days. Then he can move over to my place."

Walt started to object. He liked the idea of having a runaway slave in the storeroom; but Touss waved him silent.

"I have room to spare and no strapping son like you to help around the farm. But, Walt," Touss's expression turned serious, "I wouldn't go talking about Sunday."

"Why not? He's safe here. He can't be sent back to slavery."

"No," Touss agreed, "but he can be sent back for murder."

"Murder!"

"Maybe. Sunday is most upset about something. He keeps mimicking the firing of a gun. It might be that someone was shot when bounty hunters found them, but I think there's more to it. Sunday might've killed someone to escape."

"In self-defense," Walt said.

"But if the bounty hunters come forward, it will be their word against Sunday's and Sunday can't speak. Even if he could, the word of a black man, free or not, counts for little. So let's just keep this business to ourselves. And look out for strangers. You know how easy it is to cross that river. If smugglers can do it, so can bounty hunters, especially if they have a mind for revenge."

"All that trouble over one slave?"

"Probably not, but keeping an eye out can't hurt."

"I guess not," Walt said.

"I'd best be going. Take care of our guest. I'll drop by as often as I can." Touss's smile returned. "You can tell McKenzie, of course. I hear you two are best friends."

"I already have." Walt blushed but added, "She's promised to keep it a secret."

Touss ducked out the door, leaving his deep laugh echoing around the walls.

Walt swirled his now-cold cocoa. You simply try to help someone who falls in your lap, and all sorts of potential problems hover on the horizon. Shaking his head, Walt went to see Sunday.

They'd spread a mattress in the middle of the small storeroom's floor. The space around it was piled with sacks of potatoes and flour and bottles of preserves. Sunday was lying down but jerked into a sitting position as Walt entered.

"Hello, Sunday. How are you doing?" Walt asked cheerfully — then instantly regretted it. But Sunday didn't appear to mind. He smiled and nodded. He still had bandages on his hands and feet, but there were only a few patches of frostbite on his face — a face not a lot older than Walt's.

The pair stared at each other for a long moment, and Walt became increasingly uncomfortable with the silence. What do you say to someone who can't answer?

"I'll stoke up the stove and heat us some soup."

NATE

April 10, 1861
General Beauregard's Headquarters
Charleston, South Carolina

Nate looked at the general with awe. Pierre Gustave Toutant Beauregard. "Little Napoleon" he was called, and Nate was prepared to believe it. Like his namesake, Beauregard wasn't tall, but he was imposing. Ramrod straight in his immaculate gray uniform, he surveyed the world through sparkling blue eyes set on either side of a sharp nose. Only his bushy mustache threatened a touch of irregularity to his well-groomed appearance.

This was the man who was about to give the order to begin the war. He had been sent to Charleston to form a "ring of fire" around the Federal troops at Fort Sumter out in Charleston Harbor. The ring was complete, and the streets of Charleston were alive with the tramp of marching feet, the pounding of drums and the crack of muskets fired enthusiastically in the air. On every street corner, orators harangued eager crowds on the desirability and inevitability of war.

On their way to meet the general, Nate and his father had stopped their carriage to listen to Congressman Roger Pryor of Virginia shouting from a hotel balcony at an enthusiastic mob. Pryor was a firebrand who had once challenged a fellow congressman to a duel. He had journeyed to Charleston to see the war he so fervently wished for become a reality.

Nate had been surprised at how young Pryor looked — no more than thirty, he judged. Lank, dark hair lay plastered across his wide forehead. A large nose sat above a mouth that, when his lips were still, formed a hard line. But those lips were rarely still as Nate and James had watched over the heads of the crowd.

"You have at last annihilated this cursed Union, reeking with corruption and insolent with excess of tyranny," Pryor had said to thunderous cheers. "Thank God it is at last blasted and riven by the lightning wrath of an outraged and indignant people. You in South Carolina have bravely led, but my own dear Virginia will surely follow. And I will tell you, gentlemen, what will put her in the Southern Confederation in less than an hour by the Shrewsbury clock — strike a blow! The very moment that blood is shed, old Virginia will make common cause with her sisters of the South."

The stirring call — "Strike a blow!" — had rung through the streets just as "Dissolved" had four months earlier. It rang through Nate's head now as he stood as close to attention as he could in Beauregard's office.

Nate's father shook hands with the general. "I have brought you my son, Pierre," he said formally. "He wishes to do his part for the South. I ask you to take good care of him in this coming adventure."

General Beauregard was a family friend. Nate's mother's family and Beauregard's family had been quite close, and there had been many visits to the plantation house in the years before Elizabeth's death. James didn't host many social functions now, but the general had ridden by just last month to pay his respects when he had been appointed commander of Charleston Harbor.

"I shall do that gladly," Beauregard said, transferring his gaze to Nate. "He shall be constantly by my side. If this trouble lasts long enough, we shall teach you the business of war. Eh, young Nate?"

Nate took the offered hand and attempted to respond to the firm grip.

"Always grip a hand tightly," Beauregard said, "even if you are terrified of the man who offers it. A good grip is a sure sign of a good man. That's your first lesson."

"Yes, sir," Nate replied.

Beauregard smiled. "Don't worry, James," he said. "I will look after him." Turning to Nate, he added, "These are hard times, young Nate. We must all do our duty as we see fit. I pray that this unpleasantness will be resolved without cannon fire, but I fear it will not. So we must all busy ourselves in training and preparation. Are you ready?"

"Yes, sir," Nate said a bit louder than he had intended.

"The first thing you need is a uniform. I will have my batman kit you out, and we shall find a place for you on the staff." Beauregard turned back to James.

"Be certain that he will turn out splendidly. A credit to Elizabeth's memory and to the South. Now, you must excuse me. There is much to be done."

James looked at his son standing self-consciously in his best clothes beside the neat little general.

"Make me proud," he said gently, before stepping into the outer office.

"Yes, Father," Nate said to the retreating back, his voice thick with emotion.

Two days later, as the first pale light of dawn suffused the sky above the masts of the Union ships waiting off Charleston Harbor, Nate watched Roger Pryor step out of the small boat onto the pier at Fort Johnson. He had just been rowed from Fort Sumter, where Major Anderson and his 128 Union soldiers and civilians had refused Beauregard's surrender terms. Pryor looked much smaller than he had on the hotel balcony.

"Come on, boy," he said to Nate, who sat uncomfortably in his brand-new uniform, "let us get this over."

Beauregard had sent Nate to accompany Pryor and Confederate officers to the fort.

"Be clear on this," the general had stressed. "Give Anderson every chance; but if he refuses our terms, we must fire on Fort Sumter. At dawn, the signal will be given from Fort Johnson."

"I request the honor, in the name of the Confederate States of America, of giving that order." All eyes had turned to Pryor at that moment. He was volunteering to go down in history as the man who began the war.

"Very well, Mr. Pryor," Beauregard had said. "As you wish."

Pryor had looked triumphant — this was the blow he had shouted should be struck. Now he hesitated on the dark, wet steps of the landing. Nate hung back. Was he having second thoughts? There would be no going back once the first cannon fired, and the way forward was dark and uncertain. Pryor turned as if to reboard the boat, then stopped.

"Can I do it?" Pryor's voice wavered. "It is what I want. What I have worked for these past years. But now, when I think of all the blood that will flow from this first cannon shot …" His voice trailed off as he looked around at the deeper shadows. "Can you see them?"

Nate looked, but could see nothing but darkness. "What?" he asked.

"Ghosts. Thousand upon thousand of them. Women — mothers — begging for the lives of their sons who are going to die."

Pryor let out a long sigh that seemed to shrink his body. Then he shook his shoulders as if to shake off the ghosts. His decision was made.

Striding into the fort with Nate in tow, he faced the commander, Captain James. "I cannot fire the first gun of the war," Pryor said.

James nodded. He turned to his aide and said, "Lieutenant Farley, be so kind as to make the mortar ready for firing."

Pryor and Nate hurried out of the fort and reboarded the boat to return to Charleston and report to General Beauregard.

Nate was trying to understand what he had just witnessed. All the excitement of being a part of history had vanished, like the ghosts Pryor had seen. This should have been a glorious moment. It wasn't fair to have the thrill taken away. Nate felt cheated. He wanted to leap into this great adventure. Instead, something that should have been so simple had been made complicated by Pryor's weakness.

A few minutes into the harbor, Pryor ordered a halt. The boat drifted silently as the men watched the dark shape of Fort Johnson. After what seemed an eternity, a bright flash lit the sky. It was followed by a low, thundering roar and the red light of a fuse.

The light rose impossibly high in the sky, hung for a long second and then began a leisurely descent onto Fort Sumter. High above the fort, it exploded in a cascade of sparks. Almost immediately, other cannons opened up from the forts on the shore. A sheet of flame seemed to engulf Fort Sumter.

Pryor's body sagged as the crew recommenced their rowing. "What are we doing?" he mumbled amid the roar of the shells.

But Nate felt a surge of joy. This was it — war! The birth of a new nation — the Confederate States of America. Nate's nation. A cause to fight for.

A shiver passed down Nate's spine. What wonderful times he lived in. Here he was, in at the beginning and, he promised himself, he would be in at the end.

May 20, 1861
Montreal, Canada East

A woman burst from the low door of the mud building and raced across the dry ground. Her clothing was disheveled and bloodstained and her mouth open in a scream of horror.

Immediately, three dark-skinned, half-naked men converged on her flight. They waved cruelly curved swords, and their faces were twisted into grotesque masks of hate. All three swords descended simultaneously, driving the woman to the ground. The swords rose and fell again and again.

The figures stopped. With a low whirring noise, the men glided backward to their starting places. The woman, resurrected from her terrible end, rose and hummed her way back to the hut and through the door.

"That is the House of the Ladies at Cawnpore. After treacherously betraying the garrison and slaughtering the men, and as General Havelock's relieving force approached, Nana Sahib ordered the brutal massacre of over two hundred defenseless women and children in the house you see re-created accurately before you. The killing took hours, and several of the murderers had to leave the building to replace swords that had broken in their hellish work. Afterward, the floor of the house was found to be six inches deep in blood.

"The pitiful bodies of the unfortunates, some still living, were then dragged out and hurled down the well you see in the foreground. The well was filled to within four feet of the top and, it is said, strong-stomached soldiers who had fought in many a battle were unable to look into its depths.

"Now, if you will proceed around to your right, you will experience the valiant Relief of Lucknow."

Mr. LaRue's Mighty Panopticon of the Recent Sepoy Rebellion in India was everything Walt had hoped. It was all here, portrayed by more than eighty thousand moving models of people and animals on a vast circular table. Around it, visitors stared in open-mouthed awe at the Relief of Lucknow, the Siege of Delhi, the Tragedy of Cawnpore. Vast panoramas of battles and massacres vied for attention with smaller scenes of almost unbelievable courage and luck. Cities burned with sparking red fire and drifting smoke, columns of men marched and charged over a dusty landscape, cannons roared and the wounded screamed as brave and faithful servants loyally spirited their European sahibs and families to safety. Walt was having the time of his life.

Walt gazed at his mother as she rustled along in a storm of lace and silk. It always amazed him how many clothes city people wore. On the farm you chose clothes because they were comfortable, hard wearing and more or less clean. Walt always felt scruffy in the city.

"How horrible!" Emma moved around the exhibit, holding a lace handkerchief to her face as if the smell from the well at Cawnpore, on the other side of the world, could reach her delicate nose.

Walt smiled briefly at the thought before the opening cannonade of the Relief of Lucknow drew his attention back to the Panopticon.

❖❖❖

Walt had not stopped talking about the wonders of the Panopticon since they had left the glorious finale and found this small tearoom. Between amazed recollections of what he had seen, Walt gulped from a glass of lemonade while Emma sipped daintily from a china teacup.

Kenneth had left them and gone to conduct some business of his own. He often left the pair together on these visits to Montreal. He told Walt it was so that the boy could get to know his mother, but Walt had seen the sad look in Kenneth's eyes when they were all together and suspected that the separation was as much for his father.

Still, Walt could usually persuade his mother to take him to something interesting — there was always something to do in the city.

"Those poor women and children," Emma said. "Why can't wars be limited to the soldiers who want to fight?"

"Father says wars have a way of getting out of control once they start," Walt said.

"He would," Emma answered as she nibbled on a dainty. "Your father always sees another side to everything. That is one of the most exasperating things about him. Nothing is ever black and white.

"But then soldiers always want to fight. There wouldn't be wars if they did not. Look at all the men rushing to join the armies in America. Even Canadians are going, and it's none of our concern. As soon as anyone says 'I am going to form an army to attack someone,' thousands of men flock to fight."

"But aren't some things worth fighting for?" Walt asked.

"Oh, don't get me wrong," Emma said quickly. "Men should be allowed to have wars — it is in their nature. I just don't think women and children should be involved. If generals want to have a battle, they should all get into their grand, colorful uniforms and find a big field somewhere and fight it. After a day or two, a winner would be declared and everyone could go home."

Emma always had such different ideas — that was one of the things Walt liked about these visits. He didn't think this idea was very practical, but it did make him think.

Walt's mother interrupted his thoughts with a surprising question. "Are you going to join the army?"

He had been thinking about the adventure — half-formed thoughts of gallant charges, glory and honor. But he had never asked himself the question quite so directly.

"I don't know."

"I just wondered," Emma said casually. "So many young men are, at the moment."

"Would you be cross if I did?"

"Cross? No, not cross. I would worry, of course, but you are sixteen now, and you must go your own way and pick your own dangers. I long ago gave up any right to determine what path you would take." A flicker of sadness crossed Emma's delicate features. In a soft voice, she began:

"*The bursting shell, the gateway wrenched asunder,*
The rattling musketry, the clashing blade;
And ever and anon, in tones of thunder,
The diapason of the cannonade.

Is it, O man, with such discordant noises,
With such accursed instruments as these,
Thou drownest Nature's sweet and kindly voices,
And jarrest the celestial harmonies?"

"Is that one of your poems?" Walt asked.

"Heavens, no." Emma shook her head gently. "What do they teach you in the country that you don't recognize Henry Wadsworth Longfellow?"

"Is he a friend of yours?" Walt tried again.

Emma smiled. "I see I have a lot of work to do on your literary upbringing. Longfellow is an American poet, although he lives in England. You might enjoy his work. Some of it is robust enough for your taste.

"But enough of this war nonsense. Tell me about the unexpected guest you had over the winter."

Walt outlined Sunday's abrupt arrival, his recovery and his move to Touss's farm. "Touss is teaching Sunday to write, but it's slow. His hands are almost better now, but it's awkward always having to find paper or a slate whenever he wants to communicate the simplest thing."

"I suppose in this wilderness you inhabit, you are so out of touch that you have never heard of Mr. Gallaudet's system?"

Walt gazed blankly at his mother, unsure whether he should answer yes or no.

"Well, it's quite the thing," Emma continued enthusiastically. "There are schools teaching it all over. It has been created for deaf people, but anyone can use it. I will bet we can find a book on it at Mr. Barris's store."

"What is 'it'?" Walt asked in confused frustration.

"Why, it's a system for talking with your hands. They call it American Sign Language — it was changed from the French — and it is quite wonderful. To see someone proficient in it is truly amazing. Their hands fly hither and thither, yet another who knows it can understand every word as if the person was speaking English."

"So, using this system, someone who can't speak and someone who can could learn this language and talk?" Walt could suddenly see a way to talk to Sunday without him having to write down everything.

"Of course," Emma went on. "I shall buy you a book this very evening. Now, what shall we do with the remainder of the afternoon?"

"Well," Walt said hopefully, "the newspaper was advertising Mr. A.J. Davis as 'The Man Born without Arms, Thighs or Knee Joints.' He might be worth seeing."

Emma groaned. "You are a cause lost to the finer things in life, young Walter," she said. "But let us go and see your Mr. Davis."

WALT

June 16, 1861
McGregor Farm
Cornwall, Canada West

Sunday and Walt sat on the porch as the late afternoon sun painted the world a rich gold. Across the King's Highway, the distant river glistened. Carts and carriages rumbled or rattled past, throwing up small dust clouds that swirled in the breeze. The road to the farm, outlined by rough, split-rail fences, curved lazily up past the cowshed to the house. Beside the cowshed, McKenzie slowly chewed her cud and regarded the two figures on the porch with idle curiosity.

It had been a perfect summer day, warm and clear. Kenneth had gone to town to pick up supplies, and Sunday had walked over from Touss's farm for his lesson. On Walt's lap lay an open book, the pages filled with drawings of hands, the fingers curled in a variety of shapes. Beneath each sketch was a letter of the alphabet. The book had arrived in the mail two weeks earlier. Despite his mother's enthusiasm and promises, it hadn't been possible to pick up a copy of the sign language book while Walt had been in Montreal, but, true to her word, Emma had ordered one and mailed it to her son. Both Walt and Sunday were progressing with sign language whenever work allowed them to get together.

"Z," said Walt, pointing to the picture in the book. Sunday copied the gesture. "Now we can talk," Walt said. Then he repeated it with his hand, "N ... o ... w w ... e   c ... a ... n   t ... a ... l ... k." It was a laborious process, spelling the words out letter by letter with many hesitations to check the book, but when Sunday replied, "Y ... e ... s," Walt felt a thrill pass through him. It would be a long time before they could communicate comfortably and about complex things, but not having to rely on chalk and slate was a great achievement.

Putting the book aside, Walt lifted his notebook and moved on to the next stage of the lesson — spelling. The pages of the notebook were filled with neat rows of printed words.

"Where did we get to last time?" Walt asked running his finger down the list. "We did 'Canada' and 'hello.' Let's try 'good-bye.'" Walt looked up, and formed his fingers into the letter "g." But Sunday was staring down the drive at two figures on horseback who had turned off the road and were cantering toward them. Walt sensed his friend tense.

"What is it, Sunday? Who are they?"

In answer, Sunday leaped to his feet and fled around the side of the house. The two men spurred their horses on. At the foot of the porch steps, they split, one going to either side of the house.

Walt sat, stunned by the strange events. Eventually, he went down the steps and followed where Sunday had gone. He was almost knocked over by the returning horsemen dragging a limp Sunday between them.

"What in hell is going on?" Walt shouted angrily. "Who are you?"

The two men dropped Sunday in the dirt and looked down at Walt. One was bareheaded and sported a thick beard. The other had a thin, sly face and wore a misshapen black hat with a wide brim. Both were covered in dust and wore large revolvers on their hips. The sly-looking one carried a long whip coiled over one shoulder.

"What do we have here?" the man with the whip sneered. "A young pup with a liking for runaway slaves. Well, this un's mine, and I aim to take him, so you'd best just stand back and forget you ever seen us. That way, you won't get hurt none."

"Who are you?" Walt asked again.

"I beg your pardon," the sly man said. "In all this excitement, I must have forgot the formal introductions." The man removed his hat with an exaggerated flourish. "My name is Frank King and this here's my compatriot, Jake Stone. We are here on legitimate business, so don't get in our way."

"What business?" Walt demanded.

"Well, boy, this here slave," King gestured at the prostrate Sunday, "is a runaway and we aim to take him back. Now, Jake," King said, turning to his companion, "why don't you just truss up our catch and we can be on our lawful way."

"No!" Walt was surprised at how firm his voice sounded. Inside he was quivering like jelly, but he stepped forward until he stood between Frank King and Sunday's prone body.

"My, my. We've got a brave little pup here," King said, sliding the whip off his shoulder.

"You won't get away with this." Walt tried to make his voice sound defiant, even though all he wanted to do was run. "You're bounty hunters, and we don't tolerate bounty hunters here."

King guffawed. "Do you hear that, Jake? They don't tolerate no bounty hunters. Well," he went on, uncoiling his whip, "do you tolerate murderers?"

Walt's brow furrowed in puzzlement.

"Yep. This here black that you seem so fond of is a murderer. Just last winter I saw him put a bullet through my old friend Jesse. Threw him clean into the fire. Time we got Jesse out, weren't more'n a crisp left. I would call that murder."

"That was self-defense. Sunday was being kidnapped."

"Wrong again, boy. 'Tain't kidnapping to return a slave to his rightful owner. I am within my rights to fetch him back."

"You are not within your rights in Canada."

"Heck, Jake. Are we in Canada? It's so hard to know exactly where you are in all this country." The whip flashed out and cracked loudly in the air beside Walt's ear.

Walt shivered but stood his ground. "You have no rights here," he said. "Besides, you cannot even prove this man is an escaped slave."

"Now there you are wrong, boy. I've been hired to recapture this runaway, and he bears his owner's mark. Look on his right shoulder."

Walt hesitated, puzzled.

"Go on, look. You will see the initials of his owner."

Walt bent and carefully slid the tattered shirt off Sunday's shoulder. Amid the dirt were the angry weals of a brand — "JMG."

Walt stared in horror at this barbarity. Someone had held a red hot iron to Sunday's skin so their ownership of him could be seen forever.

"Enough," King snarled. "I mean to take this man back with me and collect my bounty. So you can stand in my way and suffer the consequences, or you can step aside and let me go about my business."

Walt shook his head. "Go to hell!"

A look of intense anger crossed the bounty hunter's face. He raised the whip high and back. Walt wanted to cower and beg not to be hit, but he stood still and closed his eyes. The whip flicked out in preparation for the cut.

"I wouldn't do that if I were you."

Walt jerked his eyes open at the familiar voice. His father stood at the corner of the cowshed beside McKenzie. He held a double-barreled shotgun, pointed at King. "You touch my son and it will be the last thing you do. Drop the whip and get down off those horses. And keep your hands well away from those guns."

The whip fell into the dust and the two men dismounted sullenly.

"Walt," Kenneth ordered, "kindly relieve them of their sidearms."

Legs shaking with relief, Walt lifted the revolvers from the men's belts. He was surprised at their weight.

"Now," Kenneth went on in a more relaxed tone, "Walt, you attend to Sunday while I lock these boys secure in the cowshed." Waving the barrel of the shotgun, Kenneth shepherded the two men toward the shed.

As Walt bent over Sunday, Frank King growled, "You ain't seen the last of me, boy. Don't you go forgettin' me, 'cause I ain't about to forget you. There's some cuts of the whip I owe you, and I aim to pay double."

WALT

June 17, 1861
McGregor Farm
Cornwall, Canada West

"They *what?*" Walt was incredulous.

"They let the two men go on condition that they return across the border and never set foot in Canada again," Kenneth explained patiently.

They were by the cowshed. Walt held a pail of McKenzie's milk and Kenneth stood beside him, the reins of his horse in his hand. It was evening, and he had just returned from Cornwall.

"But why?"

"A number of reasons," his father said. "Sunday wasn't seriously injured. No great harm was done —"

"No great harm?" Walt shouted indignantly. "Only by good luck. They knocked Sunday unconscious with a pistol butt, and God knows what else they would have done to get him back across the river. They were about to whip me. They should be sent to prison."

"I agree. But the world isn't perfect, especially now. We mustn't give the Union an excuse to go to war against us. Those two men could have been that excuse."

"But they had no right —"

"Yes, we both know that, but there will always be folks who'll twist things around to suit their purposes. Frank King was only doing what he was hired to do a little overenthusiastically, to be sure — but legitimate under American law."

"It's ridiculous," Walt said sullenly. "How did they find us anyway?"

"That was lucky —"

"Lucky!"

Kenneth held up a placating hand. "Lucky for Touss," he said. "Apparently, King and his companion knew about Touss's house being a safe house for runaways. They figured that was where Sunday was. They were heading there when they spotted the two of you sitting on the step."

"How's that lucky?"

"Well, if they had made it to Touss's house, he would probably be dead."

"Dead!"

"He was no use to King — he isn't an escaped slave — and I cannot see Touss standing calmly aside while they took Sunday. He would have fought, and I suspect King would not have thought twice about killing him."

Walt fell silent. It could all have turned out much worse. "Do you think King'll try again?"

Kenneth shrugged. "It would be stupid of him, but he struck me as a man who bears a grudge, so there's no telling what he might do. We'd best all be on our guard." Kenneth hesitated, then went on. "I'm proud of you. The way you stood up to those ruffians. It was very brave."

"I was really scared," Walt said, feeling the color rise in his cheeks.

"So was I," said Kenneth. "Standing by that shed, facing two armed and desperate men, and with you stuck in the middle. I was terrified."

"You didn't look it."

"No? I'd been scared ever since I saw them riding up. It didn't look right, so I dismounted and crossed the field on foot to see what was going on. I took the old shotgun I keep in the buggy." Kenneth thoughtfully chewed his lip. "You know what, though? That shotgun I waved about so confidently? It wasn't even loaded."

"What?"

"I'd used the last shells on a brace of grouse a couple of weeks back." Kenneth looked a bit sheepish. "I had been meaning to replace them, but just never got around to it." Walt nodded, still stunned.

"Anyway," Kenneth continued, "bravery doesn't mean anything if you are not scared. True bravery is overcoming feeling scared and still doing the right thing. And that's what you did."

"Thanks," Walt said. "When I saw the brand on

Sunday's shoulder, I was so angry, I just   It's as barbaric as cutting his tongue out."

Kenneth looked thoughtful. "Apparently Sunday escaped from a plantation outside Charleston in South Carolina. He traveled a long way. King was the plantation manager there before he took up a bounty hunter's life. He has a grudge against Sunday because Sunday shot one of his men when they attacked the runaways' camp last Christmas."

"So Touss was right — Sunday did kill someone."

Kenneth nodded. "It was King who branded Sunday after a previous escape attempt. The owner's initials let people know where to send him if he ever escaped again.

"Strange, though, the plantation is owned by a man named McGregor. King said that's what 'JMG' stands for — James McGregor."

"Angus and Lachlan lived near Charleston."

"I doubt it's our relatives," Kenneth said. "It's a common enough name. Lots of Scots settled around there.

"But enough speculation. Take the milk in and get some supper on. I'm famished."

NATE

July 21, 1861
Henry House
Bull Run, Virginia

Nate was fascinated and terrified.

He was fascinated by the panorama of war spread before him. From the summit of the hill where he stood, he could see a vista of rolling fields sprinkled with ragged clumps of trees and men in blue uniforms. Some marched in solid masses, some in thin skirmish lines, others as individuals or pairs, but all were working their antlike way closer to Nate. Here and there, still shapes dotted the landscape, marking where earlier attacks had failed. White, puffy clouds showed where shrapnel shells exploded in the air, and dark gouts of earth indicated explosive shells. Cannonballs bounced over the ground like demented bowling balls, and musket shot sped overhead. Around Nate, spread along the crest of the hill, gray uniformed men were returning the enemy's fire.

All this Nate regarded with interest. What terrified him were the noises. Muskets cracked with a sharp report, and the balls whizzed through the air with an annoying hum. Cannons barked and shells exploded with a deep roar that shook the earth. Every sound signified death or wounding, and the boy found himself jumping nervously.

What was worse was the background noise, sometimes swamped by the loud crashes, sometimes clearly audible, but always present — the human sounds of battle: the shouts of the officers, the yells of the charging men, the screams of the wounded. The guns were discrete, either close or far away, but the human noise was everywhere, like a fog of anger and suffering through which Nate had to find his way.

Nate wished he were back behind the hill, safe in the deep ravine, beside the imperturbable General Beauregard.

It was early afternoon, and things were not going well for Beauregard's army. The Yankees were attacking in increasing numbers, and the Confederate line was weakening. As Nate had climbed to the summit, he'd passed a steady stream of soldiers heading down to the safety of the rear. Some were wounded, holding blood-soaked rags to gaping wounds or shattered limbs that Nate tried not to look at. Many others just looked stunned, with glazed expressions and vacant eyes. Many had even discarded their rifles.

Beauregard had ordered Nate to climb the hill, find General Bee and discover what was going on. Trying his best to ignore the cannonballs, the shrieks and the advancing line of blue-coated soldiers, Nate forced himself along the crest.

He passed Thomas Jackson, sucking slices of lemon as he calmly ordered his brigade of Virginians to fire at this or that target. He saw Bee in the distance, on horseback, behind his soldiers' firing line. Soldiers were drifting back past him, and he was surrounded by a disheveled tangle of men who milled around indecisively looking for guidance. Bee was frantically calling for them to return to the firing line and hold off the coming Union charge. But the steady flow continued. Nate swallowed hard, struggling to resist the urge to join the stragglers and run as hard as he could back down the hill. He approached Bee, pushing his way through the disorganized knot of men.

"General, sir," he said as loud as he could, "General Beauregard's compliments. He wishes to know how the men are holding."

"Son," Bee said sadly, "tell General Beauregard that they are not holding. They are running. In fifteen minutes, there will not be one Confederate soldier on the brow of this hill. Tell him that these farm boys are not soldiers yet, they can take no more. All my officers are dead or wounded, and I can find nothing more to inspire these men. You tell him that."

"Yes, sir." Nate turned to go, relieved that he could now retreat honorably.

"One moment, son." Bee's voice stopped him. "You came by Jackson's brigade?"

"Yes, sir. I did."

"They are the center of the line. How did they seem to you? Steady?"

"Yes, sir," Nate replied, "very steady. They are solid and holding well."

Bee looked thoughtfully through the battle smoke toward Jackson's brigade. Then he looked back at Nate. "Well," he said, "if Jackson can hold, so can we." Standing up in his stirrups, Bee called out to the men around him.

"Look!" Bee yelled. "There is Jackson standing like a stone wall! Rally behind the Virginians!"

Automatically, heads turned to stare through the smoke, and gradually men drifted back to the firing line. Still waving encouragement to his men, Bee looked down at Nate. "Never underestimate the worth of a ringing phrase," he said. Then Bee gasped sharply. For an instant, he appeared frozen, like a statue in a town square. His sword fell to the ground and a puzzled expression formed on his face. In a rush, he exhaled, a gout of blood welling up his throat from the hole the musket ball had torn in his stomach and lower back. The blood sprayed over Nate, splattering his face and jacket. Still looking confused, Bee began to slide out of the saddle. The bloodstained form loomed over Nate like a horror from a nightmare come to crush him. He panicked. The noises overwhelmed him — he was going to die.

Nate ran.

He ran back along the crest of the hill, past
Jackson's men firing at the advancing Union soldiers,
toward a small two-story house, the only refuge in
sight. Nate burst through the door and up the stairs. It
was only when he found there was nowhere else to run
that he leaned, gasping, against the wall.

The window at the end of the hall was broken, and
the walls were pockmarked by stray musket balls. The
floor was strewn with shards of broken glass and plaster
dust. Three doors led off the hall, two closed, one ajar.
On the wall hung a child's needlepoint sampler bearing
the legend "Home Sweet Home, Judith Henry, aged
10, 1786."

The sounds of battle were muted by the house
walls, and Nate felt safe. He knew it was a false security
— the house announced itself as a perfect target for the
Union gunners — but just having something solid
around him helped quell Nate's terror. Until a voice
came through the open door.

"Who's there?"

Nate flattened himself against the wall.

"Who's there? Come on, speak up. I know you're
there." The voice was not threatening, just curious, and
it sounded old and quavery.

Nate took a step toward the door. "Nate Mc-
Gregor."

"Well, Nate McGregor," the voice went on, "come
in here and let me get a look at you."

Cautiously, Nate edged closer and peered in. The
room looked miraculously untouched by the battle.

The window was intact and no bullet holes scarred the walls. A huge brass bedstead took up most of the floor space, the headboard positioned against the wall across from the door. In the bed, almost lost among a voluminous pile of pillows, lay a very old woman in a fancy white bed shawl and knitted cap. A gnarled walking stick lay along the blankets beside her.

"Well, come in, come in," she said. Nate stepped forward until he stood at the foot of the bed.

"I'm sorry," he said, "I didn't know anyone was in the house."

"Never heard of knocking first?" Before Nate could answer, the woman continued, "I suppose you are part of that nonsense going on outside?"

"Yes," Nate answered, although he didn't think of it as nonsense. "I am with General Beauregard."

The old woman weakly waved a scrawny arm. "General This! General That!" she said scornfully. "What do I care for generals? All they do is cause trouble and nuisance and get young men such as yourself killed for no good reason that I can see."

"But we are fighting for a state's right to secede," Nate said indignantly.

"A state's right to secede," she mimicked. "Grand words, sure enough, but what do they mean to me? I'll still be here in my bed whether Virginia is part of the Union or the Confederacy. And all those young men out there will be just as dead."

Nate was trying to think of something powerful to say about what he was fighting for when a musket ball crashed through the window and tore a long gash in the ceiling. Instinctively, Nate ducked as a fine rain of plaster dust wafted around him.

"Ha!" the old woman laughed. "It's too late to duck once you hear the ball."

"You should leave," Nate said angrily. "It's dangerous here."

The woman laughed again. "At my age," she said, "it's dangerous anywhere." Her eyes sparkled with life in the midst of the wasted, impossibly wrinkled face. "Son," she went on, "I was born in this very room in the same year as this country. I've seen wars and soldiers come and go, and I ain't never seen the need to leave my house. This latest brouhaha is no different.

"Now, Wilmer McLean down the road, he left. Upped his entire family, left as pretty a brick house as you could want and skedaddled south to some God-forsaken crossroads called Appomattox Court House. Says to me he was finding someplace safe from the war. 'Wilmer,' I told him, 'you give this war enough time and it will reach into your parlor at this place you're running to. This is my place and I aim to stay, come hell or high water.'

"Besides, young man, do you expect the battle to halt while all you brave and strong soldiers carry an old woman to safety? I'll take my chance here. If the Lord decides that this is my time, then so be it. I've seen enough for this life."

"You're Judith Henry," Nate said, remembering the sampler on the wall outside. Another musket ball thudded into the outside wall of the house.

"Indeed I am. Although, if this goes on, I don't know how much longer that will be true. Now, you get on back down and go on doing whatever it is you're supposed to do in this muddle."

Nate hesitated. He considered carrying Judith Henry downstairs with him. As if reading his mind, the woman went on, "No, I ain't going anywhere. You get on though. Git!"

Reluctantly, Nate stepped back into the hall. He was already out the front door when the shell exploded. The noise deafened him, and glass from the shattered window rained down. Without thinking, Nate rushed up the stairs two at a time.

The hallway was a chaos of plaster and swirling dust. The door to the bedroom hung outward at a crazy angle. Pushing it aside, Nate re-entered the room. A hole had been torn in the wall, and the bed had been thrown violently on its side. From beneath a pile of bloody pillows, a wizened arm protruded at an impossible angle.

Nate backed out the door, tears streaming down his face. Why her? What harm could an eighty-five-year-old woman do anyone?

Gently, Nate took the sampler from the wall and removed the cloth from its frame. He rolled it neatly and tucked it into his pocket. Then he went back down the stairs and rejoined the war.

July 26th, 1861
Manassas Junction, Virginia

Father – I am alive.

There were times yesterday when I was sure I would never write those words. It is afternoon and my hands have only now stopped their shaking. I have seen things that I will spend the rest of my life trying to forget. Real battle is so different from my imaginings.

But having come so close to death, I feel more alive than I ever have before: the sun rose brighter this morning, the greasy bacon for breakfast tasted richer, my thoughts soared in a way I could not have imagined possible.

I am alive!

And we won. We were forced back by the Yankees within an ace of breaking, but we did not. They did, and to see them flee back to Washington – soldiers all mixed in with the dandy congressmen and their fancy ladies who had sallied forth to see their glorious army rout the rebels – brought a cheer to all our lips.

Lincoln's abolitionist boys ran home with their tails between their legs. That will teach them to meddle with the South! Secession is safe. There are those who were all for charging after the Yankees, but we were fair done ourselves and it has turned to rain today, so the roads are hopeless. In any case, we do not want Washington, just to be allowed to do what we wish in our own homes. They cannot deny us that after this great victory.

In an odd way, I shall be sorry that there will be no more fighting. Despite the horrors I witnessed, I would do it again. I know now why there are wars – to fight in a battle and to survive! I am different, not only from the person I was two days ago, but from the mundane mass of humanity that has never done nor seen the things I have done and seen.

Does that sound arrogant, Father? It is how I feel.

Your soldier son,
Nate

WALT

August 25, 1861
McGregor Farm
Cornwall, Canada West

"The harvest looks to be good this year," Kenneth said.

Walt and his father sat by the parlor fire on Sunday evening, the one break from the work week in the fields. "It has been hard this year, but with a good crop and prices going up because of the war we should come out of it all right."

Walt just nodded tiredly.

"If we have good luck with the weather, then we shall be able to —" Kenneth was interrupted by a knock at the door. "Who could that be at this time of the evening?"

He picked up the lantern and crossed the room. Walt watched the flickering light move into the hall and heard the front door open.

"Why, Touss, and Sunday," his father exclaimed. "What brings you here? Come in and sit." The light returned, followed by his father and two figures, caps in hand.

"No, no, Mr. McGregor," Touss said. "We just stopped in to say good-bye."

"Good-bye?" Kenneth asked. "Why good-bye?"

Sunday signed excitedly.

"What's he saying?" Kenneth asked Walt

"He says, 'We're going to join the army. We're going to fight for freedom,'" Walt said, translating Sunday's rapidly moving hands. Sunday had taken to sign language well. He still slowly spelled out some words, and his spelling was very eccentric; but he knew the signs for most things and concepts. Walt and Touss were less proficient, but they could always be lazy and resort to speech.

"We have thought on this long and hard," Touss explained. "This war amongst the states may seem to be about secession, but it is really about slavery. Mr. Lincoln has suggested as much. It seems to me and Sunday that that is something worth fighting for. I am told there are agents in Montreal who can arrange sign-up and passage to New York. Black men are allowed in the Union Navy, and we hear that the Union might raise a unit of free black men. We aim to be a part of that unit." Touss grinned.

"When do you leave?" Walt asked.

"First light tomorrow," Touss answered. "We are all packed. We plan to ride to Montreal and sell the horses.

With that, the money from selling the livestock and what I have saved, we'll have enough to travel where we need to."

The shadows of the four figures flickered over the walls. No one seemed to know what to say. Eventually, Touss broke the silence.

"I want to thank you, Kenneth. You have always been a good friend and a help when a body has needed it. There is some feed over at the farm and the little crop we planted this year. You and Walt are most welcome to whatever you can find. We plan to return when this is over, but who knows when that might be. In the meantime, please treat my piece of land as your own and do with it whatever you see fit."

"Thank you, Touss," Kenneth replied. "I shall care for the farm. When you return, it will be as ready for you as if you had never left."

"Thank you again."

"Yes, thank you," Sunday signed to Walt.

"You're welcome, Sunday. Good luck."

"Yes, the best of luck," Kenneth added. "It is a brave thing you are doing, and I admire you for doing it. If there is anything you need — anything at all — just ask."

Touss shook his head. "We will manage just fine. Now, we had best be going. It will be an early start tomorrow."

"Of course." Kenneth stepped forward with the lantern. "I'll see you out."

Walt watched the light retreat to the door.

"Wait!" he shouted suddenly. Walt picked up the sign-language book from the table in the corner and handed it to Sunday. "You'd better take this. It might come in useful."

Sunday made the sign for "thank you" again, and they were gone into the night.

Walt and Kenneth returned to the parlor.

"I wonder if they know what they're getting into?" Kenneth asked thoughtfully.

"An adventure," Walt responded.

"I suppose if I had been a slave, it is an adventure I would wish to be a part of."

"Do you think *we* will be a part of it?" Walt asked.

"I hope not. Lord Palmerston seems keen to keep the Empire out of the war for practical reasons. There are very few British regular troops here in the colony, although two thousand more have been sent over."

"I wonder what it's like to be in a battle," Walt mused. "I've read that people feel much more alive and aware afterward."

"That's probably true," Kenneth agreed. "Of course, feeling anything is the luxury of those who survive. It is only the living who write the stories."

"I suppose it must be like I felt after Frank King was here — thrilled and scared all at once."

Kenneth looked long and hard at his son. "Life on the farm must seem pretty dull with all that's going on in the world."

"I'm too busy to think it's dull." Then, lowering his eyes, Walt said, "But, yes, thousands of Canadians, and now Touss and Sunday, are off to war. In a way, I envy them."

"I suppose there is no point in telling you not to envy the discomfort and marching and bad food?" Without waiting for an answer, Kenneth asked, "Are you thinking of joining the army?"

Walt's head jerked up. "Mother asked me that question, too. I've thought about it, but I'm scared of going off to a foreign country and joining up with people I don't know. It would be easier if Canada was forced to go to war."

"Don't wish for that. And don't be impatient. There will be plenty of time to make a decision in a year or two.

"If you do eventually decide to go, I will not be happy. I will probably try to talk you out of it, but I shall respect your decision and not stand in your way. I only insist that you talk it over with me before you decide. Deal?"

"Deal." Walt felt a weight lift from his shoulders. Oddly, his father giving him permission made going less attractive. "Thank you."

"Everybody's thanking me this evening," Kenneth said with a laugh. "It makes me nervous. Now go bed down McKenzie — and don't spend half the night talking to her."

October 23rd, 1861
Centreville, Virginia

Father,

Your letter has finally arrived after traveling over much of the Confederacy.

Since Bull Run, we have sat in frustrating inactivity. From our forward posts – I have visited them – one can look across the Potomac River and glimpse the building works on the dome of the Capitol Building in Washington. It is odd to think that I can look upon the half-finished roof beneath which Lincoln sits. If only we could fire a shell that far. But we cannot. Our guns are not large enough and, in any case, many of them are merely tree trunks painted black – Quaker cannons, they are called – to fool the Yankees into thinking we are stronger than we are.

General Beauregard devises grand plans for circling Washington and drawing the Union into a pitched battle beyond its fortifications, but we lack the men. President Davis was here for a conference and promised to do what he can, but there are simply not enough men or guns to defend all the Confederacy. We must keep a large army in the west to hold Fort Donelson, else Nashville will fall and the South will be open by the back door. It is all so frustrating, and this is telling on the general. He is unwell, being subject to fits of fever and melancholia.

At least we have the victory at Ball's Bluff to cheer us. It was not a major battle, but we whipped the Yankees and took over 700 prisoners, more than the number we killed at Bull Run. Word from our spies in Washington is that the news of the defeat caused considerable consternation. Good.

Well, I must leave off now. It seems that we are busier when not fighting than we are in the midst of battle. There are so many small and tedious details to be attended to.

I hope you are well.
Nate

November 6th, 1861
Philadelphia

Mister Kenneth and Walt,

I ~~rite~~ write to you as best I can to tell you of our ~~jurny~~ journey and adventure. It is not easy for me to write but Touss is helping.

We ~~is~~ are here in this ~~grate~~ great city and have had a much easier journey down than I had the other way. We ~~has~~ have found no black soldiers yet but we still look. Many ~~foks~~ folks ~~has~~ have helped us when we tell them all we want is to fight to end ~~slavry~~ slavery.

This writing is very hard as Touss must tell me most ~~evry~~ every word so that I can write this letter well.

I hope you ~~is~~ are both keeping well. Touss sends his best. I will write more when I can.

Sunday

WALT

November 20, 1861
McGregor Farm
Cornwall, Canada West

"It's going to be war?" Walt asked from the kitchen doorway, unable to hide his excitement.

"Looks like it." Kenneth was sitting at the table, a newspaper open before him, his clothes steaming away the early snow that had settled on them on the ride back from town. "One thing guaranteed to set the drums beating in London is interference with one of Her Majesty's ships on the high seas, and that is exactly what some hotheaded Union captain has done.

"Apparently HMS *Trent* was carrying two Confederate ambassadors to Europe to win support for their cause. A Union boarding party removed the ambassadors. Since Britain is neutral, many see it as an act of war. Unless Lincoln returns the two Confederate ambassadors and apologizes immediately, which I cannot see him doing, the prime minister will declare war against the North. Lord Palmerston is said to have ten thousand regular soldiers preparing to sail for a march on Washington. We may soon be allies of the South."

Walt had wanted war to save having to make difficult choices, but now it looked as if the British Empire would be fighting on the side of slavery — on the same side as Frank King and against Touss and Sunday. No, Walt would be fighting to stop Cornwall and the rest of Canada from becoming part of the Union. That was what he had to think of, because the idea of war *was* exciting. The bursting shells, rattling musketry and clashing blades in the poem his mother had recited to him rang in Walt's ears.

Perhaps his mother was right. It was his nature to go to war and fight.

"Don't go rushing off now," Kenneth said, as if reading his son's mind. "Nothing will happen before the spring at the earliest."

Walt looked up. His father suddenly looked much older. Walt felt a pang of guilt at leaving him to run the farm alone. But what choice would he have?

"I won't do anything before spring," he promised.

Kenneth nodded. "Having no choice doesn't simplify anything — it just alters the complexities. When you get to my age and have seen as much of war and rebellion as I have, you will realize that. I know it seems that you're missing all the adventure — it is difficult at your age not to be a part of what is going on."

"How do you know?" Walt interrupted, angry at his father's condescension. "You're far too old to fight in war."

"But I wasn't always," his father said quietly. "When the War of 1812 began, I was pretty much your age."

"But you didn't fight."

"No," his father admitted, "but I wanted to, probably just as desperately as you do."

"So? Why didn't you?"

Kenneth was silent for a long moment, but Walt didn't want to break the mood. At length, Kenneth spoke. "I'll tell you a story that I have never told anyone. I have never told it because I was, and am, ashamed of what I did. However, I think it might answer your question about why I didn't join the army.

"When the Americans invaded in 1813, they came ashore just downstream from here. That was when Touss ran to tell the British the news.

"The Americans occupied Cornwall — it was little more than a village then — and most of the farms hereabouts. We had an American officer billeted here on the night before the battle at Crysler's Farm. I can still see him — tall, fair hair and bright blue eyes. He looked very grand in his uniform with its shiny buttons and epaulets.

"He was very polite and gentlemanly, always with a kind word for me. He called me Jock, because of our Scottish ancestors. But I hated him. He was an invader. I wanted to kill him for that, so I wished I was a soldier.

"They were unstoppable. They would tear into the infantry and destroy the British line. At that moment I loved those dragoons for their beauty and bravery and hated them for invading my land.

"But then an amazing thing happened. The end of the British line, which had been facing away from the charge, wheeled around like a well-oiled machine and discharged a volley of concentrated musket fire into the oncoming Americans. Horses tumbled, men were thrown or blown out of their saddles. I am certain men were screaming, but the only sounds I could hear over the guns were the horses — an almost human scream but higher in pitch. Unearthly. It sent shivers along my spine.

"The charge collapsed in less time than it takes to tell you about it. The survivors straggled back, leaving dead and dying horses and men on the field. The superb training of the British regulars had won the day. I was exultant. As I trekked home through the woods, I decided I would become a soldier as soon as possible."

"But, Father, I thought you said the battle stopped you from becoming a soldier?"

"I'm not done yet," Kenneth said grimly. "I was sneaking back through the trees when I heard a voice. 'Jock,' it said faintly, 'is that you?'

"I froze. The voice was very close. 'Jock, if it is you,' it said, 'come close. I cannot hurt you. I am gravely wounded and would ask for your help.'

"The voice was so pitiful that I overcame my fear. The officer who had been billeted with us the night before was behind a bush, propped against a tree. He had obviously dragged himself there, but how, I had no idea. One arm was missing entirely, and the other was severed at mid-forearm. Both wounds were ghastly — red, torn meat and white, shattered fragments of bone. The officer's uniform and a large area of the forest floor around him were soaked in blood. A sickly sweet smell wafted through the air, and already the flies were crawling over his wounds.

"'Well, young Jock,' he said, laughing softly. 'I don't look too good, do I? Have you seen the battle? How goes it?'

"I told him what I had seen and that we had won. The officer smiled again. 'That is the way war goes,' he said, 'but I fear it will make no difference to me. I am done.'

"I offered to get a doctor, but he declined. 'My only choice is whether I go quickly and cleanly or let those butchers at me and linger in agony for a week or two.' He looked at me intensely. 'Perhaps you can help me,' he said.

"'Look in my belt,' he said. 'Do you see the pistol?' I nodded. 'Good. It is loaded and primed. Would you carefully remove it please?'

"Thinking that it was causing him discomfort, I gently pulled the pistol out of his belt. It was not a pleasant task as the handle was sticky with the man's blood, but I soon had it in my hand.

"'Now listen very carefully, Jock, and do exactly as I ask. Cock the hammer back, place the barrel against my forehead and squeeze the trigger.'

"'No!' I shouted in horror.

"'It would be the greatest favor you could do me. I cannot live long, and even if I could, I would not want to without my arms. All I can look forward to is a time of agony, and I do not know if I can stand much more. The pain comes and goes. It is easier now, but it will return, and I dread that more than all the battles I have fought. I beg you. Do this one thing for me. I shall be grateful and bless you for it. Will you do me this one great favor?'

"I don't know how long I stood before the man, my thoughts a turmoil. I had dreamt that very morning of killing him, but dreaming a thing and doing it …

"It was the returning pain that decided me. His face creased and his breath became ragged and labored. All the while he kept his eyes, with their silent appeal for mercy, fixed on mine. What remained of his one arm flapped in a grotesque parody of beseechment.

"The click as I pulled back the hammer was deafening. The officer smiled at me. Slowly I raised the pistol. 'That's it, Jock,' he said through clenched teeth, 'gently does it. Against the forehead now, nice and firm. Almost there.'

"My hand was shaking so much that I could barely hold the pistol steady, but he calmly talked me through it. Once the muzzle was against his head, I hesitated. 'Come on now,' he encouraged. 'That's right. I'll say good-bye now, and thank you, young Jock.' Then he closed his eyes and I pulled the trigger."

In the silence, Walt noticed that a tear had formed in his father's eye. Kenneth wiped it away with a shaking hand.

"I ran home without a care for who might hear or see me. My parents were wild with worry, and the first sight of me didn't help. My clothes were torn where I had caught them on thorns, and filthy where I had fallen to the ground. I was covered in bruises from falls and was crying uncontrollably. They consoled me, but despite all their pleadings, I never told them what had happened that day. I never told a living soul until now, but not a day has gone by that I have not thought of the look in that dying officer's eyes and what I did."

"But what choice did you have?"

"Perhaps none," his father replied. "I could have dropped the pistol and run away, but I would have spent my life haunted by the agonies I had left him to endure. Instead, I remember killing him. Who knows which is worse?

"I was damned whatever I did. Anyway, that afternoon cured me of any desire to join anyone's army. After that, I saw the wild, futile charge of the American dragoons not as glorious but as dozens of repetitions of the tragedy I had been a part of in the woods."

"But there are good reasons to fight," Walt said, struggling to make sense of what his father was saying.

"Yes," Kenneth acknowledged with a nod, "and repelling an invader or destroying slavery are two of the best. But my point is that war, however noble the cause, is fought by individual men and must, therefore, ultimately come down to countless individual tragedies such as the one I experienced. Fighting for a just cause does not make it any easier to kill another human being face to face.

"We may go to war over the *Trent*, or you may decide to go and fight against slavery regardless. Whatever happens, temper your thoughts of glory and great causes with the memory of the American officer I killed."

Kenneth stretched to pull himself out of his morbid mood. "We have the winter ahead of us. Let us hope it brings an end."

NATE

December 31, 1861
McGregor Plantation
Charleston, South Carolina

"Is General Beauregard keeping you busy then?" James asked his son. The pair were sitting before the fire in the sumptuous parlor.

"Oh yes," Nate replied. "There is always so much to do. But it is good to get back to decent food and a comfortable bed for a few days. Although, to be fair, being on General Beauregard's staff allows for more comfort and privilege than the average soldier gets. Still, it is field duty and therefore lacks the comforts of home."

James nodded. "And you are enjoying the adventure? Your letters suggest so."

"I am. Much of the work is dull, but the excitement at other times makes it all worthwhile."

Nate hadn't told his father the details of Bull Run or about Judith Henry. He couldn't tell anyone, but he kept her sampler with him at all times, his good luck charm.

Sometimes Nate would wake in the middle of the night and see Judith Henry's old, smiling face floating in the dark. It wasn't frightening, but it did disturb him somewhat. Oddly, now that he was back in the safety and comfort of home, the images of war so flooded his brain that he was looking forward to going back to the bustle and simplicity of army life.

"Well, I am proud of you," his father said, raising his crystal glass in a toast. "I thought the war would be over by now, but the Confederacy has acquitted herself well. Our victories show that we are easily a match for the Yankee armies, and the *Trent* affair brought Britain within an ace of joining us. I am sure all of Europe will recognize us if they have another year without cotton. Then the North will be forced to negotiate an end to this business." James took a long drink. "Meanwhile, Nate, do your duty. Bring honor to the family and the Confederacy."

"I will, Father," Nate replied awkwardly. He knew his father meant well, but the past eight months had distanced them in a way that could not be bridged. James had never been to war and knew nothing of it other than what he read in newspapers. Nate knew that the papers told a story well short of actual events. He sighed. Home was not turning out to be the pleasure he had dreamed of in his cold wintry billet in Centreville.

Something else was bothering Nate. His father had lost weight and didn't look well. He was tired and lethargic, and his aristocratic cheekbones now seemed to be pushing through the wrinkled skin. And James was drinking a lot. Nate rarely saw him without a glass in his hand, even before lunch. His father had shrugged it off as overwork, which made Nate feel guilty for going off to war and leaving the entire plantation on the old man's shoulders. But Nate worried that it was more than that.

The plantation did not appear to be doing well — there were fewer slaves doing less work. Once immaculately kept paths were sprouting weeds, and sheds that had gleamed looked in need of paint and repair. Even the plantation house looked sad and unkempt. His father said it was because of the Union blockade — the European countries might eventually be forced into war for lack of cotton, but in the meantime James couldn't sell any. But Nate was sure there was more to it. His father didn't seem to care anymore.

"Nathaniel." James interrupted his son's thoughts. "Tomorrow you will be off again to God knows where. I am sure Pierre will give you leave when he can, but this is war and it may be a long time before you return. Who knows what will happen." James hesitated as if unsure how to go on. "I am not a young man anymore, and I do not know how much more time I will be blessed with." James hurried on to stall his son's protest. "It's true. Old age comes to us all — if we are lucky.

"I have made as many mistakes as the next man, but there are two I regret more than the others. The first is not making more of an effort to reunite the family."

"You mean Great-grandfather Rory's descendants in Canada?"

"I do. It has been almost eighty years since Lachlan and Angus fought. I daresay your cousins are, by now, unrepentant abolitionists who want nothing to do with us, but it has been long enough. It is too late for me, but I want you to search them out after this war is over."

"We both shall."

"Perhaps." James smiled weakly. "But if not, will you?"

Nate nodded, but before he could add anything, his father went on. "My other regret is hiring Frank King."

"He was a brutal man. We are well rid of him."

"It is not his brutality I regret, although he did sometimes overstep. I am afraid I gave him more responsibility than his competence or honesty warranted. After your mother died, I lost interest in many things. I was happy enough to pass over the running of the plantation to King."

"It does not surprise me that he was incompetent," Nate said.

"He was competent enough, but at lining his own pockets. It was only after he left that I discovered by how much."

"Then we are well rid of him," Nate said again.

"Yes, but his legacy remains." James paused and drained his glass. "If this war goes on and the blockade is not broken, the plantation will not survive another two seasons."

Nate sat in shock. The plantation couldn't fail. It had always been there and always would.

"I had hoped," James continued, "to pass it on to you one day. But now ..."

"We'll manage," Nate said almost desperately. "I won't go back. I'll stay here and help you run the plantation."

"Thank you, but that will not help. It is out of our control now. Besides, you must go back — you made a promise to General Beauregard. But should anything happen to me, I want you to sell the place to the Heywards."

"No!" Nate exclaimed. He half rose, but his father waved him back.

"It is the only way. I have discussed it with them. I know they have airs, but they are family by marriage and they will pay a fair price and clear our debts."

"It won't come to that," Nate said angrily.

"Let us hope not. Let us pray for a great victory in the spring to show these Yankees that they must let us go our own way. Now enough of this talk. You must to bed. Be off."

Obediently, Nate rose and retreated, his head swirling with confused thoughts. At the door, he turned back. His father looked pitiful, hunched in his chair, clutching an empty crystal glass and staring into the dying fire. In that moment, a wave of disgust at his father swept over Nate. It was not disgust at his mismanagement of the plantation or any of the mistakes he had made — he could forgive his father for that. What he could not forgive him for was becoming old and weak. Coming home had been a mistake, and Nate yearned to return to the simplicity of the battlefield.

February 6th, 1862
Philadelphia

Walt,

Touss and I ~~is~~ are headed down to Kentucky where
~~Genrat~~ General Grant has gone to take Nashville
soon. It is said that he has use of black soldiers. We
thought of joining the navy but ~~i's~~ I'm scared of the
water. Touss has been teaching me to shoot. Even if
they do not give us muskets, we can be useful as
drivers and such. At ~~leest~~ least we will be close to
the fighting.

See how good my writing is getting and Touss has
to help much less now. I have also been ~~practising~~
practicing my signs, but I have found no one to use
~~them with.~~

How are you and your father? I hope you are
both as well as we are. I miss Touss's farm but this is
good work that we will be doing.

Wish us luck.
Your ~~frend~~ friend,

Sunday

WALT

February 13, 1862
McGregor Farm
Cornwall, Canada West

The first thing Walt heard was McKenzie's frantic bellowing. Dazed from a deep sleep, he wondered what was causing the flickering orange light playing on the ceiling above him — until the crackling sound gave him the answer.

"Fire! Father! Fire!" he yelled, leaping out of bed, hauling on his trousers and boots and lunging to the window. From deep in the blazing depths of the cowshed, McKenzie screamed in panic and pain.

Walt flung himself down the stairs, hurled the front door open and exploded out. Eyes fixed on the burning shed, Walt didn't see his father's body on the porch. His foot caught, and the boy tumbled down the steps. Before he could catch his breath, strong hands pinned his arms painfully behind his back.

Gasping, Walt couldn't see who held him, but another figure was clearly visible by the light of the fire. He had a thin, sly face and a long whip coiled over his shoulder.

"Frank King," Walt whispered in disbelief.

"That's right, boy. Ain't you pleased to see me?

"Jake and me was up this way on some business and, seeing as how I ain't never forgot nor forgiven yet, we thought we'd drop by and pay a social call. Besides," he added with a smile, "you're worth money now, boy."

"What do you mean?" Walt tried to sound defiant.

"Well, seems young lads such as yourself are not joining the army as quick as some of the generals would like. Jake and me, our new job is to encourage you to do so."

"Crimping agents!"

"Now, that's not a nice way to say it. I prefer 'recruiters in the cause.' And you can count yourself lucky you're too valuable for me to give you the lickin' I promised. Besides, you can look forward to eighty-five cents a day and as many Yankees as you can kill."

"Yankees?"

"Why, sure," King answered. "You didn't think I was going to sell you to some blue-belly regiment so's you could go and shoot brave Southern boys, did you? You're going to be a real soldier — one of Colonel Nathan Hanson Woods's finest."

Walt's mind reeled in horror. Not only was he being kidnapped to fight in the war, he was being kidnapped by the wrong side. It was then he noticed the body that had tripped him.

"Father!" he yelled, struggling ineffectually against the man who held him.

"Don't you worry," King said, "your pa ain't dead. He'll wake up with a mighty sore head is all."

A despairing bellow from McKenzie galvanized Walt into desperate action. He lashed out with his right foot. It connected with his captor's leg, and Walt was satisfied to hear a grunt of pain, but the grip on his arms never loosened. Fingers dug agonizingly into Walt's muscles and sent needles of pain down his trapped and twisted arms. Tears flooded Walt's cheeks as he helplessly listened to McKenzie's agonizing cries falling silent.

"Look at that," King said with a sneer. "We got ourselves a sensitive one here. Jake and I would just love to wait around here gossiping over old times and eating us a steak or two — I suspect they're just about done by now — but we have some distance to cover, and that fire is going to attract unwelcome attention, so we'd best be on our way."

King reached into a pocket, produced a bottle and poured some liquid onto a filthy rag. Walt struggled as the cloth was pushed in his face. His last dizzy vision was of the roof of the cowshed collapsing on whatever was left of poor McKenzie.

March 23rd, 1862
Pittsburgh Landing

Mister Kenneth and Walt,

We have finally joined the army. We were misled.
There are no black men fighting in the army — not
yet anyways — but we are lucky and have joined up
with the ~~sofly~~ supply column for General Grant's
army. The work is hard but I pay that no mind. I have
worked harder when I was a slave and I am being
paid now. That is what being free means, I guess.
 We are all down here at a place called Shiloh
but it is nothing but an old church. Pittsburgh
Landing is where the army came ashore and as soon
as General ~~Boot~~ Buell arrives we will march and
whip them Southern boys. I cannot wait to do my
bit, even if it is just carrying supplies. Touss says
hello. He only has to help me put some of my words
in the right order now and spell the longest ones.

I hope you are both well.
Your friend,

Sunday.

WALT

April 3, 1862
Near Pittsburgh Landing, Tennessee

The six weeks since he had been ripped from his home had been nightmarish. Walt had traveled much of the time bound and gagged, by boat, on horseback, on foot, by wagon, by train. He had no sense of the distance covered, just bone-jarring rides, the smell of horses and the rumble of freight carriage wheels beneath him. Almost all the time, he had been hidden under something, usually foul smelling. Often he had been chloroformed, giving him blinding headaches that were only now beginning to clear after several days in Confederate territory.

Walt was not sure how many crimping agents there were, but there were now a dozen captives, although none had been brought from as far away. Walt worried about his father coming to only to find the byre destroyed, McKenzie dead and Walt missing. He

would have summoned the authorities, if the fire had
not attracted them first, but there would have been
little they could have done. By daybreak, Walt had been
in America, hostile country for the Southern crimping agents, but beyond the reach of the Canadian
authorities.

Throughout the journey, Walt had learned to keep
quiet, but that had not prevented King from throwing
a sly punch or kick his way — far less than the beatings
early on, when Walt had railed against his kidnapping
and looked for any opportunity to escape. There had
been none — he was always securely tied or carefully
watched by King or Jake.

As they had passed through Yankee territory, Walt
had feared he would be shot or silently disposed of. But
now their captors were relaxed, and Walt felt they must
be close to their destination.

This afternoon, the party was sitting in a clearing,
the captives tied in a circle and the captors standing
idly, smoking and talking. All of a sudden, Walt noticed
the captors cock their heads and listen. Then Walt heard
it, too, the jingle of equipment. Mounted men were
approaching.

After a few tense minutes, a group of heavily
armed men trotted into the clearing. They wore broad
hats and gray uniforms, stained with mud and dust.
That the imposing figure on a gray horse was an
officer was just visible through the dirt that caked his
uniform, but there was no doubt that he was in
charge and the center of attention. His deep-set eyes

whipped around the clearing — Walt was certain they missed nothing.

Removing his hat, King stepped forward. "Colonel Woods," he said, "it's good to see you again."

Woods barely deigned to look down at King. "That may be, but what have you brought me?"

"Twelve enthusiastic volunteers," King replied, gesturing to Walt and his companions.

"They look none too enthusiastic to me." Woods cast a glance in Walt's direction. "But no matter, they will do. Here is your money." Woods casually tossed a bag to King, who grabbed it eagerly. Then the colonel turned to a man behind him. "Untie those men and give them uniforms. And the others, too," he added, giving King a long look.

"Beg pardon, sir," King said nervously, "but we didn't come here to fight. We was aimin' to sweep out west for more recruits."

"Well, Mr. King," Woods said, "as I see it, I have two choices. I can let you go and drink the money I just gave you and hope that, when that runs out, you can shift yourself enough to scrape up another handful of reluctant volunteers. Or I can make a soldier of you now. Since I believe the next few days will see some hot action, you and your comrades are more use to me in uniform than drunk in some Memphis tavern. All you need do is remember to obey orders. If you don't, I will personally shoot you.

"And that goes for the rest of you, too." Woods scanned the other men in the clearing. "You will ride with me wherever I go and do whatever I say. And you had best not fall behind. We do most of our work behind the Union lines, and they do not take kindly to lone graycoats. So, you can try to escape and be shot by the slave lovers, you can disobey an order and be shot by me, or you can do your best and fight for the Confederacy. If you fight, there is a chance you might live to a ripe old age. Welcome to the Confederate forces of America, gentlemen."

With a rough salute, Woods swung his horse around and trotted into the trees. A dozen of his men remained, one handing out gray jackets to captives and captors alike. Walt's jacket fitted him reasonably well, but a bloodstain formed a dark, stiff patch on the collar and shoulder.

"Now you are soldiers," the man who had handed out the jackets said. "We have spare horses for you through the trees — that will turn you into cavalrymen. As for weapons, if you don't have one, you'd best take one off a dead Yankee pretty quick. It's your good luck that there's a pile of them wherever Colonel Woods goes. Now follow me."

Walt trotted through the trees as ordered, too tired and shocked to do anything else. As the blood-soaked collar of his gray jacket chafed his neck, he reflected that, while there might well be a lot of dead Yankees around Colonel Nathan Hanson Woods, Walt's new uniform suggested that there were also a good number of dead Confederates as well.

April 3, 1862
General Beauregard's Headquarters
Corinth, Mississippi

"Do not fret, Pierre. We shall be watering our horses in the Tennessee River soon enough." General Albert Sidney Johnston patted the Little Napoleon on the shoulder. "Buell is not here yet, and Grant is not expecting us. We have enough men at last, and we shall destroy his forces in a day or two at most."

Johnston looked positively scruffy beside the neat Beauregard, but the man was a dynamo. His piercing eyes never rested as he bustled around organizing, whether it was the vast campaigns or the minute details of his army's deployment for the coming battle.

Beauregard looked exhausted. Recurring stomach problems and a year's hard campaigning had left their mark. His cheeks were sunken and his eyes listless.

"Very well, Albert," he sighed. "I shall prepare for the march to Pittsburgh Landing."

"And I shall give some thought to the order of battle. We shall confer this evening on Grant's final destruction. Until then …" With a half salute, Johnston was gone.

Beauregard sat heavily on the camp chair by the overloaded map table. Looking up, he nodded at Nate, who had been awaiting orders during the exchange between the two generals. "Well, young McGregor. What think you of our plans?"

Taken aback at such a direct question from a general, Nate stuttered, "I think … Well, that is, if Buell does not arrive …" Nate's answer petered out. Beauregard smiled encouragement. Emboldened, Nate went on. "I think we will whip them and the Confederacy will win the war."

Beauregard's smile broadened. "I hope you are right. The survival of the Confederacy hangs on what we do these next few days. Bull Run was a mere skirmish — five times as many men will fight in this place. The coming battle will not end the war, but it will decide it. If we win, we might win the war. If we lose this battle, we lose the Mississippi Valley and the western half of our Confederacy. Without that, we can only hold on as long as we can and pray for a miracle." Beauregard gave Nate a tight, weary smile. "Are you scared, young Nathaniel?"

"Yes," Nate answered.

"An honest soldier. This will be a bloody affair. If you wish, I shall release you from my staff."

"If you do, I shall join the first band of soldiers I meet and fight with them."

"Why?" Beauregard shot back. "Do you care so much for secession?"

"No," Nate said, "or rather, I do, but not enough to die for it. I have shifted for myself without a servant since I joined your staff and have spent but a few days at home since we went north into Virginia. I suppose I do not wish to let down my friends — or you."

"Or your father?"

"Of course," Nate added quickly.

Beauregard looked at him for a long moment. "He is not well, you know. He did not wish me to tell you and burden you in your duties, but given the uncertainty of the next few days ... He has a growth in his lungs. It has been there for some time, and the doctors give him but a little time."

Nate's mind reeled, remembering how ill his father had looked at Christmas. He was surprised to find that he felt angry and betrayed — angry that his father had not told him and betrayed at being left alone in such times.

"Do you still wish to stay with the army?" Beauregard asked gently.

"Yes," Nate answered rapidly. He would not use his father as an excuse to run away. In any case, Nate felt that his life and future were here, with his comrades, not back amid the murky finances and complex emotions of home. Hot tears burned his eyes. "Excuse me, sir," he muttered, stumbling from the room.

WALT

Dawn, April 6, 1862
Near Pittsburgh Landing, Tennessee

Walt's terrified heart was pounding so hard it felt as if his chest would explode. His uniform was soaked in sweat despite the chill dawn air. He was on an old roan mare, rather like the farm horses, a comfortable mount, but not much for charging into battle. And charge into battle was what he was about to do.

Nathan Hanson Woods and his irregular cavalry were spread out through some trees near the bank of the Tennessee River. In front of them, the camp of a Union baggage train was gradually materializing in the pale dawn light. Walt could see supply wagons drawn up beside the road and a line of horses farther away, by the river. A few small fires flickered fitfully outside scattered tents, and one large blaze illuminated a group of figures sleeping on the ground. Walt assumed there must be guards somewhere, but they had encountered none coming through the woods.

Walt still had no gun. He had cut himself a rough club, more for comfort than use. It was not much of a weapon against a musket or a bayonet. If Walt hadn't been so scared, he would have laughed. Here he was, about to go into battle on the wrong side, riding a farm nag and carrying the kind of weapon that hadn't been used in war for hundreds of years. But in the last three days, Frank King hadn't let Walt out of his sight. He blamed him for being conscripted into Woods's cavalry.

On either side of Walt, bits jangled softly and horses snorted quietly. Clouds of mist hung around animals and men in the crisp air. Beside him, King whispered, "You'd better pray that you can club a Yankee quick and get his musket because I aim to kill you just as soon as I get the chance."

Walt didn't reply, but he shivered with more than cold. His chances of surviving this day were remote.

Nathan Hanson Woods's voice echoed through the trees. "Let's kill some Yankees." What silence remained was crushed beneath pounding hooves as the men surged forward. The rebel yell — part defiant shout, part primeval scream — rose in the air. It was a sound Walt's great-grandfather Rory would have recognized from Culloden.

Walt charged. At least his horse did, drawn forward by the rush of her companions, as her rider clung on for all he was worth. Before he knew it, Walt was in among the wagons, surrounded by running, shouting and screaming men. Bleary figures were cut down by the surging Confederate troops. Some of the attackers fired into thrashing figures trying desperately to escape from collapsed tents, while others were already hitching horses to the wagons, to drive them into the woods.

Walt took no part in the battle — it was all he could do to stay on his horse, which seemed determined to head for the large fire. All at once, a figure lunged out of the chaos and made a grab for Walt's reins. The old horse, panicked by the noise and smell of blood, reared violently, throwing Walt to the ground. Dazed, the boy struggled into a crouching position and looked around. The men by the fire were all black, and none appeared to be armed. They must be the baggage handlers or horse grooms. This was Walt's chance. Clutching his crude club in one hand, Walt began taking off his gray jacket.

"Well now. Trying to run away already, are we?"

Walt turned to see King smiling down at him from horseback, a Colt revolver pointed at Walt's head. "Here's just the chance I was praying for." King cocked the hammer. "I hope the Confederate army don't miss you too much." Walt was frozen. Time seemed to have slowed to a stop.

Then he heard a voice — "Walt!" At the same instant, a rock stung the flank of King's horse, causing it to rear.

"Damnation!" King roared.

Walt turned to see a pair of black men running

toward him. Both were dressed in Union blue, although the uniform of the man in front appeared two sizes too small for him.

"Touss!" Walt shouted. His voice was drowned by the crash of King's revolver. Touss staggered, but kept coming. The revolver fired again, but Touss was so close that his momentum carried him into King's horse. Touss dragged King off the panicked horse and into a suffocating embrace.

King was struggling, but Touss's arms were locked around his chest, pinning his arms by his sides. The revolver hung uselessly, pointing at the ground. King gasped for air. His eyes began to bulge out.

The veins on Touss's forehead stood out like knotted ropes as he slowly crushed the life out of his enemy. With a surprisingly loud crack, one of King's ribs broke. King opened his mouth in a silent cry of agony, his tongue protruding grotesquely.

All at once, Sunday was beside Walt. He grabbed the club from Walt and brought it down on King's head, crushing his skull.

The force of the blow knocked both King and Touss to the ground. King's face was oddly squint where the club had staved in one side of his head. Touss's eyes were closed.

Sunday crouched beside the bodies and unwrapped Touss's arms. King's body sagged ridiculously to one side. Then Sunday gently turned Touss on his back and crossed his arms over the two neat, round holes in his chest. All the strength was gone now. The arms that had crushed King's ribs like eggshells flopped helplessly. Touss, Walt's friend from that faraway world of safety and comfort, was dead.

Sunday looked at Walt, tears pouring down his cheeks.

"Sunday?" Walt asked disbelievingly. "Is it really you?"

Sunday nodded. "Touss dead," he signed.

Unable to keep looking at his friend's body, Walt gazed around.

The battle was over. As suddenly as they had burst from the trees, Woods's men had vanished, taking the supplies with them. Confused horses and wounded men stumbled around in the early light. Destroyed tents and still bodies lay scattered about. A few blue-coated soldiers were tying up two disheveled gray figures.

Walt was brought back by Sunday tugging at his arm and pointing from Walt's gray jacket to his own blue one.

"You're right," Walt said, "I'd better get this off," completing what he had begun when King spotted him. Beside him, Sunday was struggling to turn Touss's body over. Hauling against the uncooperative weight, Sunday removed Touss's blue jacket and draped it around Walt's shoulders. Then Sunday took Walt's gray jacket and draped it gently over Touss.

9:30 a.m., April 6, 1862
Shiloh Church, Tennessee

The army was waking up. Men were milling around the tents scattered through the sparse trees, washing in tin basins or cooking breakfast over open fires. The smell of wood smoke, mixed with bacon and coffee, wafted through the air, making Walt's empty stomach rumble noisily. Fires crackled, men talked and swore, horses snorted and stamped. In the distance, muskets cracked sporadically, but no one paid them any mind.

This was the army Walt had wanted to join, and here he was in the middle of it. And it was huge. Walt and Sunday had been walking for more than an hour, rarely out of sight of soldiers going about their business. Camps were scattered in almost every clearing in the trees, baggage wagons rumbled along the narrow roads through the woods and lone riders on important errands rode past every few minutes. A vast job was being done in an efficient and businesslike manner.

In the clearing, beside the rough road Walt and Sunday were following, stood a small log building with a cross on top.

"Shiloh Church," Sunday spelled out. "Me and Touss used to say our prayers in there. We was planning on doing it again today when we arrived here with the wagons. It's Sunday."

"So it is." For the first time in weeks, Walt knew — or cared — the day of the week. "Perhaps we can go in later and say a prayer for Touss."

Sunday nodded agreement. "First we got to find Captain Whitman. He can help you get back home."

For weeks, all Walt had thought about had been getting back to Canada. Now, all he had to do was tell this Captain Whitman his story and he would be put on a train back north. But even as he thought about it, Walt knew that was not what he was going to do. He was meant to be here. Perhaps, he thought, the fates had intervened in the person of Frank King. The notion was silly, but a part of Walt believed it.

"I'm going to fight," Walt said. Sunday looked hard at him. Walt merely shrugged. He couldn't explain it, he just had to. This was where he was supposed to be. Everything was simple at last.

Without warning, a wild yell erupted from the far side of the encampment. A volley of musket shots tore through the camp, and suddenly running figures were everywhere.

For a second, Walt looked about in confusion. Gray-coated figures were running between the tents, whooping with excitement. Across the camp, blue-coated men were frantically loading muskets and being formed into a rough firing line by a bareheaded officer sporting a rough new beard.

"This way!" Walt yelled at Sunday and headed for the Union soldiers.

The Union line straggled through the trees and what was left of the camp. Many soldiers were only partially dressed, some without jackets or boots — one with his face still half lathered with shaving soap. But there were enough of them, well enough organized, that their ragged volleys halted the wild charge. As many gray-clad bodies as blue lay among the torn tents.

"They'll be back!" the officer shouted. "If you ain't got a musket, pick one up and find a bayonet. There'll be some hot work to be done yet."

Sunday picked up a musket from a dead soldier and offered it to Walt. It was longer than the hunting guns he was used to, even without the long bayonet, but it worked the same way.

Sunday looked around for another musket as Walt took the dead soldier's powder horn and bag of musket balls. Resting the butt of the musket on the ground, he began the laborious process of loading it, tamping powder, wadding and ball down the long barrel and priming the powder tray.

The Confederates were keeping up a steady fire from the far side of the camp. The man beside Walt suddenly grunted and sagged to the ground. As Sunday grabbed at his falling musket, the soldier with the half-shaved face pushed him aside and let the musket fall. "We don't need no armed blacks — we'll fight our own battles."

"His name's Sunday!" Walt shouted angrily. "And it looks like you can use all the help you can get. Besides, black skin doesn't stop a musket ball any better than white."

The man stared at Walt for a few seconds, then shrugged. "Please yourself," he said grudgingly, and loosed off a shot at the enemy.

Walt stepped back, and Sunday bent to retrieve the fallen musket. Placing his own heavy weapon to his shoulder, Walt pulled back the hammer with his thumb. He peered over the sights, looking for a target through the clouds of black smoke drifting over the remains of the camp. All Walt could see were flashes from the muzzles of the Confederate guns. Taking careful aim at one, he squeezed the trigger. The musket kicked viciously at his shoulder. His ears rang with the noise, and grains of hot gunpowder stung his cheeks. He had no idea whether he had even come close to his target. Beside him, Sunday fired into the smoke.

Above the musket fire and the screams of men, a deeper, louder roar echoed around the battlefield. Down the line from Walt, three men took the full force of a load of grapeshot.

"Fall back!" Captain Whitman shouted. "They're bringing up cannon. Fall back!"

In surprisingly good order, considering the chaos, Walt, Sunday and the others retreated through the trees, stepping over the bodies of their fallen comrades. One, Walt noticed, was only half shaved.

I'm not scared, Walt thought, leaning against a tree to reload. This morning I was terrified, yet here I am in much worse danger and I'm not scared at all.

A musket ball thwacked into a tree trunk above Walt's head. He ducked but kept on pouring powder into his musket's muzzle.

I must write to Father and tell him I'm all right, he thought as he tamped down a piece of guncotton, dropped a lead ball into the muzzle and tamped in another piece of cotton. Squinting against the stinging smoke, Walt squeezed the trigger and sent another musket ball rushing into the smoke. *I am alive.*

NATE

11:30 a.m., April 6, 1862
Shiloh Church, Tennessee

"We'll set up headquarters in that old church." General Beauregard gestured at the log building in the clearing. The fighting had moved on, but among the destroyed remnants of the Union camp, gray and blue bodies lay intertwined in death. Mostly, the dead lay on their backs, arms spread out, as if gazing at the blue sky. Nate barely looked at them as he helped move Beauregard's equipment into the church.

Nate was elated. Johnston's plan was working. The attack had been a complete surprise to the Yankee soldiers and they were being steadily driven back. By nightfall, they would be driven into the Tennessee River. Then it wouldn't matter when General Buell turned up with Union reinforcements — Grant would be beaten and the Confederacy safe.

"I know things are going well, young McGregor," General Beauregard was saying, "but it is not yet quite time to daydream."

"Sorry, sir. I was just —"

Beauregard waved off Nate's apology. "I need a message taken to General Johnston," he said. "He's to the right, where you can hear the cannon fire. It sounds as if he is having a hot time of it. I must know if he needs me to send some of my men his way. It is easier going ahead of us, and I can spare some." Beauregard handed Nate a folded note. "See he gets this," he said, "and come straight back with an answer."

"Yes, sir." Nate saluted and headed off toward the sounds of battle. Where he could follow a road or track he did, but mostly he just worked his way through the trees. Away from the camp, the bodies were less numerous, but there were still a scattering, alone or in pairs. One's face was still half covered with shaving soap. Some had obviously died slowly, dragging themselves to a tree trunk or a small stream, and some were still alive, calling for water or help. But there was nothing more Nate could do after emptying his water bottle into the first few he came upon.

Walking wounded passed him going to the rear. They were interspersed with unwounded men who simply looked shocked. Nate ignored them all.

As the firing grew louder, soldiers going in both directions now became more numerous. When Nate asked directions, most ignored him, but enough gestured ahead for Nate to keep going.

At last he came upon a peach orchard. The trees were in blossom, covered in tiny, pale pink flowers. Musket balls tore through the foliage, sending thick clouds of blossoms drifting to the ground. It was as if the trees were snowing, or weeping, Nate thought, seeing bodies on the ground almost completely covered in blossoms.

At the far side of the orchard, General Johnston sat astride his horse, giving orders. The musket balls that filled the air and cut the blossoms were coming from some entrenched Union troops across an open field, scattered with the bodies of Confederate soldiers who had tried — and failed — to take the position.

As Nate approached, he saw that Johnston was angry. "But their position is strong," another officer was saying. "We have given the Yankees a sound trouncing. Is it not perhaps time to retire?"

"Retire be damned," Johnston replied above the firing. "I shall attack as long as there is one Yankee on this side of the Tennessee River. If we do not crush Grant today, Buell will arrive and we will lose not only this battle, but the whole of the west — and the war. Those damned Yankees behind that split-rail fence are putting our victory in doubt. I want them destroyed."

"Yes, sir." The officer saluted and turned away. Nate stepped forward. As he did so, a portion of the sole of Johnston's right boot flew off, severed by a musket ball. Johnston looked down. "That was close," he said. Then, turning to another messenger, he barked, "Tell General

Beauregard to press hard on the left. We shall outflank this hornet's nest."

"General Johnston," Nate said.

Johnston turned and looked at Nate. "Yes, boy."

Nate opened his mouth to give Johnston Beauregard's message, but he stopped in shock. Johnston's entire leg was soaked in blood and blood was dripping out his boot.

"You're bleeding," was all he could manage.

"What?" Johnston said. He attempted to look at his leg, but slipped from the saddle. Nate gazed in horrified fascination at the hole in Johnston's trouser leg. Blood was shooting out in a pulsing jet.

"The general's hit!" someone shouted. Panic erupted around Nate.

"It's his leg!"

"Fetch the surgeon!"

"His artery's severed!"

The only quiet figure was Johnston himself. He lay on the ground beside his horse, blinking slowly. Then he turned and looked straight at Nate. He smiled, then his face muscles relaxed and his eyes closed.

There was a moment of disbelieving silence, then the officer who had been arguing with Johnston turned to a messenger and said, "General Beauregard's in full command now. Tell him what has happened."

The messenger saluted and hurried away. "Now," the officer said, "let us take this hornet's nest, just like the general ordered."

Nate hesitated only a moment. He couldn't deliver his message to Johnston, and there was no need for him to return to General Beauregard. All he could do was help take the Union position across the field.

Nate found a musket lying beside a fallen soldier and joined the other men forming up for the charge. As he ran, he felt Judith Henry's rolled sampler in his pocket.

3:30 p.m., April 6, 1862
The Hornet's Nest
Shiloh, Tennessee

Walt lay down in utter exhaustion among hundreds of bodies. Some, like him, were hugging the earth to try to escape the whistling musket balls and crashing shells that had been filling the air around them with noise and death for hours now. Others were dead.

The Confederates had attacked six times, as far as Walt could remember, and it looked as if they were getting ready to try again. Captain Whitman's soldiers had joined other units along the rough fence that marked the boundary between some farmer's field and the sunken road on which they now lay, and they had driven off the attacks each time, leaving inert gray-clad bodies scattered over the open ground in front of them.

Earlier, General Grant himself had ridden by, exhorting them to hold the line at all hazards. It was a stupid thing to say, really, Walt thought. What other possible hazards could there be?

Since the first attacks, Walt and Sunday had fought side by side. Exhaustion made it automatic: load, pick a target, aim, fire, load, pick a target. Between attacks you kept as low as you could, or crawled about looking for water, ammunition or powder in the packs of your dead comrades.

Sometimes Walt wondered what he was doing here among a bunch of boys from Ohio or New York, busily trying to kill other boys from Tennessee or Mississippi. It didn't make sense. But then he would picture Frank King and Touss, or he would look at Sunday frowning in concentration as he loaded and aimed his musket. Then he would remind himself that the boys who kept charging across the field had put the brand on Sunday's shoulder and wanted to own him.

Sometimes Walt thought about his father worrying himself sick on the farm back in Cornwall. Would he ever see him again, or even write the letter he had planned only this morning?

But mostly Walt didn't think, he just did.

"Here they come again!" a voice to Walt's left called out. Walt and Sunday rose and rested their muskets on the rail fence, watching as tiny gray figures burst from the trees across the field.

NATE

3:45 p.m., April 6, 1862
The Hornet's Nest
Shiloh, Tennessee

It's my birthday, Nate thought as he raced out of the
trees yet again. I'm seventeen. Will I live to be eighteen?

In the blur of the afternoon, Nate had been part of
three, maybe four attacks. It was difficult to remember
exactly. Each attack was the same, a yelling charge
across the field as men spun and fell until the momentum was exhausted by the musket balls and a hurried
retreat was called. He was trying as hard as he could,
but Nate hadn't reached their goal — the split-rail
fence — yet, and he wasn't sure how many more times
he could make this run.

Nate and the solid mass of men around him ran
over the open ground as fast as they could. Leaping the
fallen bodies of their comrades and screaming as much

to give themselves courage as to scare the enemy, they sped for the low fence on the far side of the field. All along the fence line, small puffs of smoke blossomed. They looked harmless, but men were grunting and spinning to the ground in mid-stride. Here and there, cannons let out larger, more deadly clouds of smoke and whole clumps of men collapsed. Focusing on a single point in the fence and clutching his musket across his chest, Nate raced ahead.

He was more than halfway now, his breath coming in harsh gasps. There were fewer men around him and the yelling had quieted. The officer who had ordered the attack was leading until a charge of grapeshot caught both horse and rider and threw both down into a bloody heap.

The fence was just in front of Nate now, higher than it had looked from the other side of the field. Nate saw blue uniforms, white faces and sunlight glinting off long bayonets. He felt musket balls tug at his wide flying jacket, then he was at the fence. Taking a deep breath, Nate leaped. He felt the wooden rail below his boots before it crashed in two, throwing him to one side into a mass of broken rails.

As he rolled over, Nate saw a figure aim a musket at him. He tugged at his own weapon, but it was trapped beneath the fence remains. Bracing against the shock of being shot, he looked up at his assailant. The soldier was shorter than Nate, but he had a similar shock of red hair. And although his face was partly obscured by the leveled musket, it looked vaguely familiar.

Then a black man in a Yankee uniform crashed into Nate's attacker just as he fired. Nate had a moment of shocked recognition before a violent blow knocked his head back and everything went dark.

WALT

4:00 p.m., April 6, 1862
The Hornet's Nest
Shiloh, Tennessee

The crash of the musket happened as Sunday cannoned into Walt, knocking him sideways. Had Sunday gone insane? "What the hell did you do that for?"

Sunday's mouth was working furiously but no sound came out. He seemed to have forgotten that he could sign. Wildly he pointed at the attacker.

The Confederate soldier was lying in a twisted pile amid the demolished stretch of fence. A thick stream of blood ran from beneath the man's red hair, across his cheek and under his uniform's collar. His eyes were closed and the rage was gone from his face. He was about Walt's age. Walt had never seen him before, he was certain of that, yet he looked oddly familiar.

Walt was vaguely aware that the firing had stopped. Glancing around, he noticed a few soldiers still shooting at the backs of the retreating attackers, but most were either slumped exhausted on the ground or tending their wounds or those of their comrades.

Walt felt Sunday tug at his sleeve. He was spelling. N ... A ... T ... E.

"Nate? Who is Nate?"

Sunday pulled his jacket off his shoulder and pointed to his brand, "JMG." Then he pointed to the soldier. Gradually it dawned on Walt. This Confederate must live on the plantation Sunday had escaped from. Walt looked at the body. He was too young to be an owner. He must work there, or be the owner's son. Walt studied the face. Then, with horrible realization, he knew why it was familiar. The soldier was taller and thinner, but looking at him was like looking in a mirror.

The brand on Sunday's shoulder — James McGregor. Was it possible? Was this Walt's cousin? What had Sunday called him — Nate? Had he just killed his cousin?

WALT, NATE
AND SUNDAY

Early evening, April 6, 1862
Banks of the Tennessee River
Pittsburgh Landing, Tennessee

As a hundred questions swirled around Walt's shocked brain, Nate's eyelids flickered. "He's alive!"

"Then best get him to the rear."

Walt turned to see Captain Whitman. "We beat them again," Whitman said, "but they'll be back, and we don't want no rebels running around here when they do. You and the black take this one to the rear."

Walt was hardly aware of the Confederate artillery starting up again. "Yes, sir."

Nate was only barely conscious and seemed to have no control over his legs. "You get him on the other side," Walt instructed Sunday. Together the two half carried, half dragged their prisoner across the sunken road and into the trees. Other figures, many clutching bloodstained limbs, were drifting in the same direction. Walt heard Captain Whitman shout, "Here they come again!" but he didn't care.

———————— ❖❖❖ ————————

For two hours, Walt concentrated on putting one aching foot in front of the other. Isolated images imprinted themselves on his exhausted brain: a cluster of wounded men who had dragged themselves to a muddy pond, only to die facedown in the bloody water; a young soldier carrying his severed right arm, asking politely where the medical tent was; an officer's magnificent stallion, saddle covered in blood, eyes wild and mouth foaming as it ran back and forth through the trees.

The trio eventually reached the riverbank as the rain began. They could go no farther. In the churning, muddy water of the river, riverboats and gunboats tried to keep position as their gunners lobbed shells over the trees into the Confederate positions. Around Walt, several hundred wounded and tired soldiers lay or sat, uninterested in what was going on. Nearby, a group of officers scanned the far bank.

"Well, we've had the devil's own day, haven't we?"

Walt glanced toward the voice. The man was filthy and looked to be wounded in at least a couple of places. He was talking to an equally dirty officer with a short beard and a square, rugged face. Walt recognized General Grant from his visit to the fence.

"Yes. Yes," Grant replied, "but we'll lick 'em to-morrow."

"If Buell arrives."

"He will, and we have Whitman and the men on the sunken road to thank for giving us the time. The only part of the line that held long enough to —"

Grant was interrupted by a sound from across the river. At first it was just noise, but gradually words became clear:

"Away down South in the land of traitors,
Rattlesnakes and alligators,
Right away, come away, right away, come away.
Where cotton's king and men are chattels, Union boys
will win the battles,
Right away, come away, right away, come away.

Then we'll all go down to Dixie, Hooray. Hooray.
Each Dixie boy must understand, that he must mind his
Uncle Sam,

Away, away, and we'll all go down to Dixie.
Away, away, and we'll all go down to Dixie."

Soldiers in blue appeared through the trees, clean and fresh.

"Buell!" someone shouted.

"Let's get them across the river," Grant ordered. "Tomorrow will be ours."

"Dixie."

Walt turned to see Nate sitting up holding his head.

"They're singing 'Dixie.' We have won then?"

"No, it's Buell's men," Walt explained.

Nate looked around slowly, taking in the wounded, the river and the fresh soldiers on the opposite bank. Removing his hand from his head, he looked at his bloodstained fingers. "Where am I? What happened?"

"That's the Tennessee River." Walt's gesture took in the swirling water, the gunboats and the far shore. "You drove us right to the edge of it, but Buell's here. Tomorrow will be different. What happened is a musket ball creased your scalp. It bled a lot and knocked you out, but you'll be okay."

Nate attempted to nod but stopped quickly as pain shot through his skull. "I remember running across a field," he began slowly. "And a fence collapsing." Caked blood cracked as Nate's brow furrowed with the effort. "You tried to kill me, but —" Nate turned his head, but waves of pain forced him to close his eyes. "Sunday? Is that you? How can this be?"

Sunday nodded. He was as confused as the other two. Through all his mistreatment, he had convinced himself that he had hated everyone on the plantation. Yet, when he'd recognized his childhood friend by the fence, he had acted instinctively to save his life. Sunday began signing.

"What's he doing?" Nate asked.

"Talking to you with his hands."

"What is he saying?"

"He says that he's glad you aren't dead."

Nate looked from one to the other. There were so many things he didn't understand.

"Who are you?" he asked Walt.

"That depends upon who *you* are," Walt replied. "Is your name McGregor? Do you own a plantation near Charleston? Was your grandfather called Angus?"

"Yes to all three."

"Then I am your cousin."

"You certainly look like me," Nate said. "Your grandfather must have been Lachlan, who went to Canada."

Walt nodded, just as a Confederate shell whined over the trees and exploded in a fountain of foaming water beside one of the gunboats.

"But we can talk about family later," Walt said. "Right now we had best get you across the river to safety and a doctor."

"No!" Nate barked. "No doctor. If I go to a doctor, I'll end up in a prison camp. I have to go home. My father is dying."

"I'm sorry," Walt said. "I don't know whether my father is alive or dead. I have to go home, too."

Sunday began signing rapidly.

"He says the army is his home," Walt translated.

"We will all go our separate ways," Nate said.

"Yes, but not yet," Walt replied, standing. "You will not last long in that uniform in the midst of the Union army, I think we should take you prisoner for the moment."

"And you shall have to cross considerable Confederate land to get back north."

Sunday nodded.

"Well," Walt said, "the first thing to do is cross this river." Walt offered his arm as Nate struggled to his feet, stumbling as a wave of dizziness threatened to overwhelm him. Sunday moved in on his other side. Arm in arm, the three soldiers headed along the riverbank, away from the sound of the cannons.

HISTORICAL NOTE

The historical background to this story is accurate. At Bull Run, Stonewall Jackson got his name and Judith Henry was killed in her house by Union gunfire. At Fort Sumter, Congressman Roger Pryor discovered that starting a war is not the same as calling for one. At Shiloh, blossoms did cover the dead in the peach orchard.

As Judith Henry mentions, Wilmer McLean did move his family to what he considered to be a safer place after armies started crossing his property at the first Battle of Bull Run. And it was a safer place, until the very end. On the afternoon of April 9, Palm Sunday, 1865, General Lee signed the articles of his army's surrender and shook hands with General Grant in Wilmer McLean's parlor at Appomattox Court House. For the rest of his life, Wilmer always liked to say that he was in at the very beginning and the very end of the war.

Many Canadians (upwards of 30 000 by some estimates) joined up to fight — on both sides — in the American Civil War. Despite making a significant contribution to the war, they are never mentioned in any of the standard history books. On several occasions, most notably when HMS *Trent* was seized, Canada came within an ace of being dragged into the war. Had that happened, there would probably be more than fifty American states today.

In 1860, Canada was midway between being the twin colonies of Upper and Lower Canada and the Dominion of 1867. Some still referred to the old designations, many called it Canada East and Canada West and yet more used Canada. Sometimes the names were used interchangeably. For simplicity, I use Canada throughout, except in the chapter headings, where I use the geographic distinction Canada East and Canada West.

The American Civil War produced some great songs, many of which are still sung today. The tunes, however, were often borrowed from much older British songs, usually sung by soldiers. Echoes of these songs still remain in some of the lyrics. For example, have you ever wondered why the song "The Streets of Laredo" describes a cowboy's funeral as if it were a soldier's, complete with fifes and drums? The song that Kenneth sings on the steps of his house became "The Star Spangled Banner" during the War of 1812, but didn't become popular until much later in the century.

"Dixie" was popular with both armies in the Civil War, although the words were often changed to suit the sentiments of the soldiers.

The Americans were not the only ones who could recognize a good tune. The song that Walt is singing when he scares off Touss's deer was used in the 1890s by the Australian poet Banjo Patterson to create "Waltzing Matilda."

ACKNOWLEDGMENTS

The histories of the songs in the story and Kenneth's description of the Battle of Crysler's Farm come from Donald E. Graves's excellent *Field of Glory*. The Civil War background comes from Bruce Catton's trilogy, The Centennial History of the Civil War, and Ken Burns's wonderful television documentary on the Civil War and the accompanying book. The rest comes from my imagination, and all has again been admirably whipped into shape by Charis Wahl.